So Many Secrets:

The Promise of Zandra

Book One

by
C. D. Koehler

Illustrated by
Stacy M. Cislo

PRESS

Dedicated to

Allison and Lindsay

who over the years
gave audience to the characters
and events contained in this book,
and joyfully brought this story to life.

Table of Contents

Prologue ix
Chapter 1   Peer around the Corner 13
Chapter 2   Cirlaena 18
Chapter 3   First Encounter 25
Chapter 4   The Unveiling..32
Chapter 5   Reluctant Rescuer......................................40
Chapter 6   Perfect Alibi..47
Chapter 7   Battle and the Bailiwicks...........................53
Chapter 8   King and the Kimonos................................60
Chapter 9   Two Confessions 67
Chapter 10   Marauders of the Mind 74
Chapter 11   Creetswarron 81
Chapter 12   The Deadly Rocks......................................87
Chapter 13   Ílda-dunn Crossing 96
Chapter 14   A Hopeful Horizon 102
Chapter 15   Darkondusk 108
Chapter 16   Night Visions..117
Chapter 17   Kaleena's Hand 125
Chapter 18   The Piper's Tune 133
Chapter 19   Fears in Flight...138
Chapter 20   The Healing Waters 146
Chapter 21   Beyond the Brink 152
Epilogue 161
Maps of the Underlands 165

Prologue

Thursday, April 15, 1965 (morning)

Nearly four months had gone by since Nina Leigh Fithian received the amazing revelations. She was glad for the knowing but sometimes regretted the burden, for she knew too much. In fact, no one in Holly Mills or any other town in South Jersey had a clue of the many secrets hidden in her heart. She knew that no human had ever been entrusted with the mysteries her eyes had seen in places far, far below.

Walking alone to school that morning was unusual for her, for she was always accompanied by her best friend. The two were inseparable. However, friendship was not on her mind as her bright hazel eyes stared upward at the budding trees lining Buck Street.

Nina Leigh's thoughts drifted back to the crazy months of 1964 that changed her life forever. She remembered being lost in the basement of Laura's Dress Emporium and the eerie encounter with the beautiful blonde girl whose curious wink started the incredible adventures. She felt the rush of emotion when she first learned the secret of the ancient oak and the spiraling yueblion. Her eyes widened as she recalled the orange threat of February and the glorious night ride. She could envision beasts and beaches, twists of time, the darkness of days, and bright shadows.

Nina's gaze fell to the sidewalk, marred with cracks and smudges that formed irregular designs and resembled the last sixteen months of her life. But why was she chosen? Why not the other girls in her class? And what providential purpose brought her to the attention of the Wish-Weaver? And what was the meaning of the revelations if it meant she were the sole bearer of so many secrets? Nina pondered these questions until she heard the warning bell in front of the three-story brick building.

She dashed up the concrete stairs leading to the main entrance. Stepping in front of JoAnne Dickens and Agnetha Beck, Nina grabbed the cool metal handle.

"Do you think we'll be late?" she asked, holding the door for her two friends.

"Hope not," said Agnetha, whose blonde hair flipped as she turned to resume her light conversation with JoAnne.

Just when Nina was about to enter the school, she heard a faint but familiar voice. She turned toward the sidewalk where she thought someone had called to her. But no one was there. She stood alone between the two half-opened doors, looking about. Shrugging her shoulders, she entered the lobby and disappeared up the steps. She could not have known that soon her heavy burdens would be shared by another.

Chapter One

Peer around the Corner

Thursday, April 15 (afternoon)

Piper gripped the long wooden dowel and felt the warmth of the last girl's hands from her random swing just a minute ago. The cheers and heckles of her classmates reminded her of other occasions when the sixth-grade students played huckle-buckle beanstalk and similar games.

Nonetheless, she mustered a determination so strong she could nearly see through the scarf blindfold that imprisoned her head with its wavy brunette hair—the distinctive mark of her outer beauty.

Piper Rae Slack was not competitive by nature, but right now the urgency to deliver a good hit for the waiting watchers seemed to be her sole desire. Like a batter at home plate, she committed to a stance that would render a hit no one would forget.

The dizziness of being spun around by her dearest friend, Nina Leigh, had finally subsided. Now the pressure to produce was upon her. With thoughtful intention she took her swing. The long stick cracked against the colorful piñata, lacerating the stuffed paper pig. Candy flew in all directions as her classmates scurried about like hungry robins hunting for the morning feast.

"That was some whack, Piper," said Nina, laughing and kneeling to grab the candies and lollipops around her.

"Thanks. I didn't realize how hard I hit that piñata. I was afraid of walloping someone with that stick, especially Mrs. Chauncey!"

"Yeah. Imagine that! If you had smacked the teacher, it would've ruined the whole Easter party for sure."

As the girls gathered up the last bit of wrapped candies and chocolates, Mrs. Chauncey asked them to return to their seats for the final treat of the festivity. She asked Cynthia Wheaton and Teague Simonson to pass out the cupcakes and napkins.

"Class, the end of the school day is nearly upon us. We have just one more pleasantry to perform before we adjourn for Easter vacation. We have four April birthdays this month: Kyle Johnson, Lynne Hoyt, David Paton, and Piper Slack."

Mrs. Chauncey walked down the aisles placing a birthday candle into the rich vanilla icing of the four cupcakes. Backtracking, she lit each waxy wick. Everyone spontaneously erupted into "Happy Birthday" in one melodious round. Trying to imitate a bass singer, chubby Farley Fattrack was naturally off-key much to the annoyance of the teacher.

"And now it's appropriate for our birthday boys and girls to make a special wish before blowing out their candles," said Mrs. Chauncey.

Piper's mind swirled with possibilities. What would be a good wish, a lasting wish? How could she come up with one on such short notice? She looked over at Mrs. Chauncey's face, not able to tell if the grin bore goodwill or impatience.

Glancing down at the cupcake, she pondered. The chatter of those about her muffled her muttering. "But it's only a dumb wish. Who cares what it is?" Yet there was something Piper yearned for that was to be carefully tucked into a wish.

Piper knew that Nina was her closest and most special friend. After all, the two look-a-like girls grew up together and shared nearly everything. Still, a flicker of suspicion smoldered within her. Piper stole a glance at her friend. Yes, Nina had been cleverly concealing something from her for over a year. This was no time to waste a perfect wish, for she was desperate to know what Nina had hidden behind her smiling countenance.

Quietly Piper said, "I wish to know the truth – the truth that Nina has been keeping from me, no matter how big or how small it is."

With a curious glance at Nina, Piper closed her brown eyes and blew out the candle. The other three students did likewise. Clapping and cheering echoed off the high ceiling and rustic wooden flooring. Hayley, Nina, JoAnne, and Cynthia leaned toward Piper for a group hug.

Wrapped in her friends' arms, Piper sensed the odd feeling that someone in the classroom was staring at her. Impulsively she jerked her head toward the cloakroom doorway, only to see a blonde girl in a white bonnet peering at her for an instant and then disappearing from view.

"Nina, Hayley, JoAnne, did you see that! Cynthia, did you see the girl over there?" said Piper, pointing at the old cloakroom.

"What are you talking about?" Nina replied.

"I didn't see anything," said Cynthia, who joined the other students in a quick game. Nina and Hayley remained with Piper.

"What was it?" asked Nina.

Piper frowned. "I saw some girl with golden blonde hair in a weird hat and a blue dress at the cloakroom staring at me. Honest to Pete, it was kinda creepy too!"

"Well, maybe it's one of the girls in our class," offered JoAnne, who was nicknamed Bobby Sox. "There's thirteen of us, you know."

"No!" insisted Piper. "I know what I saw, and I know the girls in our class. It was someone different for sure."

"Maybe it's a girl from another classroom," said Hayley as she and JoAnne zigzagged through the desks and peaked into the small, cluttered storage room.

When JoAnne turned her head back to the other two girls, her deep blue eyes displayed her doubt. "No one's in here."

"Hmm. That's weird," said Hayley.

"All right then. I guess it was my imagination," said Piper, her voice quivering.

Nina was tempted to investigate the cloakroom for herself when she turned and grabbed Piper's arm. "Are you sure you saw the person you described? You wouldn't be joking, would you?"

"I'm telling you what I saw — a stranger, a girl with blonde hair and the most unusual look on her face."

"Unusual? What do you mean by that?" asked Nina.

"Well, like she wanted me to see her, but she didn't – almost like she was checking up on me to see if I were here. I felt like she was trying to be real secretive or something."

Nina's expression went blank.

"What is it, Nina? What do you know?" Piper asked. By now the other students had noticed the interaction and turned their attention to Nina and Piper.

"Are you hiding something? Do you know who it is?" Piper asked with growing impatience.

Nina's face seemed frozen; her eyes widened. Neither wonder nor worry could account for her thoughts. By now other students had nearly encircled them.

Piper shook Nina's shoulder. "What's wrong with you? And who was the girl?"

Mrs. Chauncey called to the students to assemble at the doorway for the dismissal bell. All complied, save the two best friends. Nina stared in wonder at the cloakroom.

With both hands Piper turned Nina's head to face her, whispering, "Who *was* it?"

The word sprang from Nina's trembling lips: "Arianna!"

"Arianna? Who's that?"

"Arianna Angeliqué. The Wish-Weaver was here!"

Chapter Two

Cirlaena

Friday, April 16 (evening)

The thought of the sand creature terrorizing the astro-
nauts on the lunar landscape still sent chills down
Nina's spine as she readied herself for bed. Tonight's episode
of *Beyond the Boundaries* was both scary and captivating.
It would have been better to watch the television show at
Piper's house. After all, the Slacks' finished knotty-pine

basement was a perfect place in which to watch their favorite science fiction and mystery programs. Unfortunately, Piper and her family were up in Cherry Hill to celebrate her grandparents' anniversary.

It was not even ten o'clock, yet Nina was exhausted from the day's activities, which had begun with the Good Friday morning service and brunch, followed by an afternoon of spring cleaning and window washing with her mom and her brother Lance. She didn't mind wiping the sills and dusting the blinds but grew irritated by Lance's mindless chitchat and teasing.

As she finished brushing her teeth, her eyes glanced to the right where the medicine cabinet was recessed in the wall. The mirrored front panel of the cabinet hung halfway open. The cabinet mirror and the huge wall mirror above the two sinks created an eerie effect that resembled an infinite corridor into space and time. She gazed and marveled over the myriad of Nina Leighs, thinking how the fantastic reflection corresponded to her own secret, extraordinary pathways.

"Nina, when you're ready, I'll come say prayers with you," said Mrs. Fithian, leaning her head into the bathroom doorway.

With a mouth full of frothy toothpaste, Nina gurgled, "Thanks, Mom, I'll be right out."

While she was rinsing the sink, Lance popped in and pinched her on the thigh, then flew out with lightning speed.

"Ouch! You're such a brat. I'll get you for that, you red-headed stooge."

"Catch me if you can, ninny!"

Her mom yelled down the hallway, "Would you two just get in bed already before your dad gets home? He had to work late tonight, and I'd like to enjoy just a few moments of peace and quiet with him. And remember we have a busy day tomorrow too."

Nina stomped off to her bedroom while Lance's muffled giggles could be heard as he jumped on his bed in the other room.

Nina knew her mom had entered Lance's room when all the commotion subsided. She stared at the ceiling, wondering about the previous day and the strange happening at the class party. What was Arianna doing there hiding in the cloakroom? And how was she going to explain blurting out the Wish-Weaver's name to Piper and the others? Luckily, the ninth-period bell had sounded, ending the day and the urgency to render answers to that which best remained cloaked in mystery. And fortunately Mrs. Slack was waiting outside the school to take Piper to her dental appointment.

Her mom entered the room and sat on the bed. Nina always loved hearing her mother's prayers, and she thought she would never grow too old to enjoy being tucked in.

"Dearest, may the Lord grant you the best sleep ever tonight. Dad and I love you and your brother so much." A kiss sealed the moment.

"I love you and Dad too, but Lance is another story."

"Oh, now hush," said her mother with mild dismay. "He's your little brother, and he looks up to you. Believe it or not, he loves you very much."

Nina rolled her eyes, and they both giggled, sharing a warm embrace. Her mom left Nina holding Puppie, her favorite stuffed animal, which she had since birth and would not relinquish sleeping with despite her age. Once again, her thoughts drifted to Arianna and the secrets.

Just as she was dozing off, a sharp tap on the windowpane startled her. Rising up on her elbow, she glanced over to the window. A stout silhouette danced from side to side, seemingly impatient for Nina's respond. Darting to the window, she unlocked the pane. The figure lifted the lower windowpane and clumsily crawled off the small roof and into the room.

"Edip, what in the world are you doing here at this hour?" asked Nina.

Breathing heavily while he adjusted his red conical cap, the gnome grabbed her arm and led her to the bed, where they both sat facing each other.

"Sorry to bother you, my friend, but I had no choice in the matter. I was ordered to come, and come tonight, I might add."

"Ordered? By whom?"

"Because of the crisis, members of the Royal Council instructed me to find you immediately."

"Crisis? What's going on? What could be so important to involve me? Don't you know my parents could catch you? Aren't we supposed to keep you a secret – to keep all of it a secret?" Nina looked back at the door, debating whether to lock the knob.

Disinterested in the risk, the panting gnome continued.

"Young One, you remember King Tréfon, right? Well, his only daughter, her Royal Highness Princess Cirlaena, has been kidnapped, taken from the Royal Palace next to Spoleo Hall last evening."

"The princess is gone? Who would have done such a terrible thing? Why would any gnome kidnap Cirlaena?"

"No, the princess was not kidnapped by gnomes. Grand Patriarch Feedunkulus is quite convinced the princess has been stolen away by one of our enemies, the evil kandalarians."

"What are kandalarians?" asked Nina, her eyes welling up with tears. Nina had met the princess only three times but had developed a friendship with the king's young daughter.

"They are big, ugly, vicious barbarians who use battleaxes and spiked flails. They are merciless and grabbers. After conferring with his advisers and studying the little evidence left behind, Feedunkulus is convinced that Borok of Kandalar is the main culprit behind this horrible deed."

"Who is this Borok?"

"Borok rules all of Kandalar, which is south of the First Kingdom. Kandalar encompassed all the lands eastward to the Great Telexian Divide and the northwest lands to the border of the Bedloe Abidion. We do not know how far south his dominion stretches. His throne is at Castle Darkondusk, which is near the center of his authority. It is at Darkondusk that Grand Patriarch Feedunkulus believes the princess is being held prisoner."

"But why would this Borok kidnap Princess Cirlaena?"

"From what the wise gnomes can surmise, they believe Borok is in league with Emperor Shaptillicus of the Trollian Empire. It appears that if Shaptillicus cannot defeat the gnomes directly in warfare, he will attempt to crush them, ah…us… indirectly by way of the Royal Throne of the First Kingdom."

Nina lowered her head in disbelief. The gnome's thick thumb wiped away a singular tear that streamed down her pretty freckled face. Gazing into his hopeful broad eyes, she asked, "But why have you come here to tell me of such sad things? What can I do?"

"Ah! There is something you can do, Young One. My people have revered you ever since you danced into their hearts during the 'Wind of Schully Wully' celebration last June. I asked for your help then, and I am begging for your help now."

"But what can I do? I am just a twelve-year-old girl!"

"And that is the key. You see, Feedunkulus has foreseen that a successful rescue must be comprised of a team of five, a Kimonos."

"A Kimonos? What's that?"

"It is a special group – in this case consisting of two human girls, two gnomes, and a starling. I need you to be a part of that team!"

"Edip, suppose I say yes. How am I going to get away? And what other girl is going to join me?

"Leave the alibi to me. Now, for the latter, you must bring a friend. I recommend Piper."

"Are you kidding me? Piper Slack?"

"Through foreknowledge, the Grand Patriarch has determined that Piper is the one."

"But she would be scared to death to be a part of such a rescue. Edip, she knows nothing of you or the underlands. After all I've told you of Piper, do you really think she can handle such a wild trip?"

"Believe me, when she discovers that you are going, she will join you. It has been foreseen that she will accept the challenge. But first the truth must be revealed to her."

"You mean, tell her about gnomes and down below?" asked Nina in disbelief.

"Yes! I am giving you permission to break your vow of secrecy about the underlands and me. We have to recruit her immediately. We must embark to the First Kingdom the day after Easter. That will give you time to tell Piper and time for me to arrange the journey."

Nina turned her head toward the window and gazed into the night. "I'm in. How could I turn you down, especially such a wild adventure as this?"

"Excellent! I knew you would not forsake such a dire cause." Edip stood up, straightened his baggy trousers, and faced his tired friend still sitting on the edge of the bed.

"When will you come back with more details?" asked Nina. "When will I see you again?"

"I will return with an army general on Easter Day. I will meet you and Piper inside the tree, let's say a little after two o'clock. You must tell Piper tomorrow. Be wise in the telling; she will believe and know some of the secrets."

The gnome's lips trembled as he continued. "Oh, how I wish you could have truly known Cirlaena as I have known her. She is the fairest of all creatures in the underlands."

"Edip, we will help get Cirlaena back to the kingdom. I can't imagine her locked up in some dark, dirty jail cell," whispered Nina.

With that he hugged his dear friend and scurried out the window. Leaning her petite frame over the sill, Nina watched the gnome bound toward the tall ancient oak and disappear into its enormous shadows.

The bedroom door flung open. "I heard that! Who were you talking to, sis? What's up at the window?"

Nina jerked around, her head hitting on the sash. "Get out of here! My room is none of your business!"

"I heard you talking to some guy – something about a princess and a jail. What's going on?" Lance put his hands on his hips.

Nina rushed toward her brother, who fled from the room with an annoying pitch that announced his displeasure, shouting "Mom! Mommy! I know a secret!"

Chapter Three

First Encounter

Later that night

"A re you sure there's nothing you wish to talk about?"
said Mrs. Fithian as she rose from the end of Nina's
bed and rewrapped the bathtowel around her wet hair.

"Mom, there's nothing to talk about. I'm fine. Lance is
making it all up. There was nobody in here talking to me.
After all, who would it be? And wouldn't I scream bloody
murder if a burglar were in my room?"

Mrs. Fithian turned to face her daughter, who was still sitting up in bed. "I don't know. Your brother was pretty convincing that something strange was going on in here."

"Mom, that freckle-face brat is a troublemaker. You know that. Gosh, every time I turn around he's sticking his nose in my business or trying to tattletale on me about something stupid."

"I suppose." Mrs. Fithian grinned and slowly walked to the window, which was cracked open.

Nina's heart raced. "It was stuffy in here. I had it open for a while. I guess I just didn't pull it down enough."

"Yes, I suppose so." Mrs. Fithian closed and locked the window, closed the drapes, and walked toward the door. "Goodnight, Nina."

Nina heard the slight suspicion in her mother's voice, but she had avoided being found out – at least for now. Rolling out of bed she tiptoed to the corner. Gently she lifted the wooden chair and placed it in front of the window. She sat on the plaid cushion, reached for a throw blanket, and wrapped herself within its warmth. Petite fingers pulled back the long drapes; she peered into the night.

Moonlight filled the backyard with the magnificent tree as a surreal backdrop. While staring out at the immense branches, Nina's thoughts drifted. She remembered that fateful day when she first met the amicable gnome over a year ago. It was an exceptionally cold morning—just a month after the Wish-Weaver had granted her the most remarkable wish on her eleventh birthday on January 2, 1964.

She recalled being awakened out of the most peaceful dream by a horrible rumble. She saw pictures moving from side to side on the walls while the swag lamp by the cherry dresser swung like a lazy pendulum. Even sitting up in bed she felt the strange vibrations. Suddenly the quaking ceased, and was followed by squealing, grinding sounds like a distant train braking in a subway tunnel. Jumping out of bed, she changed clothes and dashed throughout the house. Alone, she grabbed her winter coat, gloves, and boots and ventured out the front door. All appeared normal except for an unusual tint to the February morning sky.

Pondering the matter, the girl sat on the frosty steps, looking around the neighborhood, which was oddly devoid of any activity. A white mail truck rolled down the street, not stopping at any residence for deliveries.

But something was wrong. The truck was not *really* speeding away. At least that is what she thought at first. Standing to get a better view, Nina squinted to see what clearly defied the laws of nature. As the truck traveled down Wisteria Way, it never changed. Nina knew that as an object moves away from an observer, the distance makes the object appear smaller. But this was not the case.

Mystified, she picked up a fallen branch on the frozen ground. Throwing the rotting wood high above the brown lawn, she watched as the branch remained the same size. Nina was now both frightened and confused. She dashed into the house to call Piper, but the telephone line was dead. Even the power was out.

Nina ran out the kitchen's sliding glass door and headed for the ancient oak tree in the backyard. As she hid under its immense branches, suddenly she felt a nudge from the bark of the tree. A small door carved into the thick, rippled bark had cracked open, revealing a face obscured by the darkness within.

"Who are you?" Nina asked, her voice quavering.

An elf-like man in drab brown baggy clothing and a strange cap partially emerged from the opening. He shielded his eyes from the bright sunshine.

"I am Edip," he offered with an unfamiliar accent. At Nina's puzzled look, he continued. "It is pronounced *eh-DEEP*. I am a gnome from the underlands."

The curious but startled girl took a step back. "I, I'm Nina Fithian. I'm eleven, and I live over there in that white house."

"Well, Nina, I am so very glad to meet you in person after all this time. You have no idea how I have longed to talk with you. For some time I have watched you play here in this very yard. At last we meet!"

"You mean you've been watching me from this tree?"

"Yes. And I must admit that in all my many years, I have never seen anyone quite as unusual and full of life as you. You are one special human girl!"

Flattered by the comment, Nina smiled and peered at the stranger. He was slightly shorter than she and rather plump. Bushy brows and long lashes adorned the fellow's squinting eyes. His age was indistinguishable, yet his furrowed forehead suggested middle-age.

"Are you a leprechaun or a dwarf? I mean, can you do magic or something like that?"

The gnome chuckled. "No, I am afraid not, Nina— although I do know many secrets. I even know some of the great mysteries of the centuries."

Nina stepped closer. "Well, I happen to love secrets and mysteries. My friends tease me all the time. My mom calls me Miss Curious. So, can you tell me a few of these secrets you know?"

"Ah!" said Edip, raising one brow. "To know any of the secrets would make you quite unique. I do not know if you could handle such things."

"Please," insisted Nina. "I must know more. I can take it."

"Well, the price of knowing is a burden to bear. You see, if I should disclose anything to you, then you must never tell a single soul. And such knowledge and burdens could overwhelm one's soul."

Nina's countenance fell. She did not understand that which she was asking. Nonetheless, she persisted.

"You say you have seen me and know me a little. Well, suppose I make a promise, take an oath not to ever say anything – cross my heart and all. Would you then trust me enough to tell me?"

Edip paused for what seemed like an hour to Nina. He scratched his beard and turned his head toward the tree's interior.

"Come inside." The gnome entered the darkness, and Nina followed behind. When her eyes adjusted to the small room, she saw a large hole on the opposite side.

"What is that?" she asked, pointing toward the railing encircling the hole. The gnome lifted a glowing device from a wall bracket and leaned over the railing.

"Please shut the hatch completely and come see."

With a trembling hand, Nina closed the small door and inched across the dank, hollow trunk. She looked down. The gnome's luminar could not pierce into the darkness more than thirty feet.

"This winding stairway is called a yueblion. It was built by the Lúboffs and Ŷvódees centuries ago. But the Ancients have moved far below to avoid the dangers."

Nina's mouth gaped open. "Dangers? What dangers?"

Edip ignored her comments. "This is the pathway to so many secrets."

"But where does it go?"

The gnome sighed and grinned. "It leads to magnificent mysteries far beneath the surface – to the underlands, to the world of Gilacia."

He sat by the cool railing and told her that he dwelled on the outskirts of Gnomen City, the capital of the First Kingdom of the Gnomes. His sketchy description of the underlands and the other regions surrounding the kingdom drew wild fascination in the girl's mind.

Nina interrupted. "Oh, did you feel the earthquake when you came up the yuebli—ah, the steps? Did you notice anything weird happening this morning?"

"Before you go off on some crazy theory, let me tell you what really happened," said Edip with a smile. He broke a twig and stuck it in the corner of his mouth. "You see, Young One, the Intra-Global Engineers who regulate the rotation of the planet's core had to make a minor adjustment during the noxx. Folks in the uplands have no idea about this except for the radical effects that occurred. But fear not; all is well! Even now things are returning to normal."

"But tell me more about the ancient people and the dangers."

He stood and guided her toward the doorway. As he inched open the hatch, light flooded the interior.

"You asked many questions. The next time we meet, I will explain much more to feed your hungry mind. Be calm. Your curiosity and courage are your strengths. Patience and wisdom will be your guides in time. I will see you again, even sooner than you are expecting, my dear Nina. Now hold my hands."

Nina reached out to grasp his callous, stubby fingers. The gnome gave her a serious gaze.

"Promise me that you will say nothing about what you have seen today to any human – to anyone! Promise me that you will keep the gnomes, the yueblion, and the underlands a deep secret."

Nina looked into his squinting eyes, took a deep breath, and sighed. "I swear with all my heart!"

Edip smiled. "Good. I trust you because I know you. And, by the way, not one word to your friend Piper."

"But how do you know—?"

"Not a word!"

With that, he smiled and disappeared behind the opening.

Reflecting on the momentous morning brought a smile to Nina's face. She looked down at the deep shadows in her yard and closed the drapes. Climbing back in bed, Nina curled up under the covers and fixed sleepy eyes on the photograph of Piper and herself at Memorial Park last summer.

"Good heavens, how am I supposed to tell Piper? How will she understand about their world?" she said to herself. These thoughts troubled her into the night.

Chapter Four

The Unveiling

Saturday, April 17 (morning)

It was not necessarily how he said it but what he said; Lance savored tattling on his sister. At least that's what Nina thought most of the time. The end of her fork dipped into the golden, syrupy pieces of waffle she had cut from the stack. Unkind thoughts of her brother played through her mind as she stabbed at the stack again and again. Her eyes darted across the table at the redheaded rascal who kept brushing aside the tail of his Davy Crockett hat.

Mrs. Fithian stood at the stove pouring batter into the waffle iron.

"Mom, I'm full," said Nina, standing to clear her dishes. "I don't think I could eat another bite. Where's Dad?"

"He's upstairs getting ready. He'll be down soon. Lance, would you like another waffle while I'm still cooking another batch for your father and me?"

"May I have one more?" asked Lance, his mouth full from the last bite.

"Of course. Now, Nina, Dad and I have to go to the bank today to settle things on the mortgage for the cottage in Sea City. We also have to run some other errands this afternoon. So will you keep an eye on things around here?"

Nina placed her plates in the sink and turned to her mother with a scowl. "What about Mr. Raccoon Hat over there?"

"He's going over to play with Robert Abel till suppertime. So you'll have the house all to yourself."

"Yeah! And away from you, Miss Smarty-Pants Ballerina," snapped the eight-year-old with a ghoulish grin.

"Oh, you big goon," Nina growled as she left the kitchen.

At the bottom of the steps, she paused, sensing the eeriness of the moment. Carefully, she climbed up the right margin of the stairway, grasping the banister to steady herself. It had been a little more than nine months since her incredible experience on the alien beach with the unthinkable juggernaut.

"This is not the time to fall through the steps into another dimension," she muttered under her breath.

She could hear the hum of her father's electric razor behind the bathroom door down the hall. Stopping, she turned into the master bedroom and picked up the decorative beige telephone usually reserved for her parents' convenience. Her slender finger spun the rotor dial. Piper answered.

"Hi, twin!" Nina whispered. "Say, my parents will be gone this morning and some of the afternoon. I'll have the house all to myself. How about coming over for lunch?"

"Sounds good. Let me clear it with my mom. If you don't hear from me right away, I'll be over in about an hour. I have to finish cleaning my room and practice my piano lesson," Piper said.

"See ya soon, Piper Rae! Bring over your bike. We may want to go for a ride later."

Gently replacing the receiver, Nina slipped into her bedroom and continued reading the novel that was due for a report when she returned to school after the vacation. She loved each page of the mystery about the castaway on the lonely Pacific island.

Just after her parents left, Lance slammed the backdoor shut and scampered to the Abels' house. Nina was tempted to yell, but only Bailey the beagle would have heard her annoyance. She placed the book facedown on the bed and pondered how to tell Piper about the gnome's unusual request. How would her best friend react to the truth about the underlands? How would she respond to Edip? And what would happen when Nina explained about the rescue?

Later the doorbell rang, followed by Bailey's howls. Nina gave Piper a warm embrace and led her to the kitchen, where they made a quick snack for lunch. Afterwards, they walked out onto the deck and over to the swing set in the far right corner of the yard. Swinging and singing, the two friends laughed while exchanging parodies to old camp songs.

"That must be one of those new 707 jets way up there making that white streak beyond the clouds," said Nina, straining her head back and shielding her eyes from the noon sunshine.

"I'd love to be up there now," said Piper. "I wonder where they're going. Maybe some place far away. What do you think?"

"Piper Rae, I bet they're going to Bermuda or the Bahamas, or maybe even Europe. Lucky them!" Nina paused and stopped swinging. She looked intently at Piper and smiled. "Would you like to go someplace special – I mean *really* special?"

Piper could tell something was different in her friend's countenance. She nodded.

"Follow me." Nina walked over to the old oak in the middle of the backyard boundary. Leaning the flat of her hand against the rough, weathered bark, she said, "See this huge tree? It holds so many secrets – mysteries I've kept from you for a long time 'cause I was forced to"

"What? I mean, how can this big old tree hold a mystery? I don't understand." Piper's brown eyes widened.

"Come sit with me by the bushes."

They nestled themselves amidst the line of arborvitaes and a stately oak that bordered the woods.

Nina continued. "You see, this old tree has a hidden opening. If I push the little bark-like knob on the side over there, the hatch will open. Piper, the tree trunk is hollow. Inside is a room with a stairwell that leads way down to an underground world called the underlands or what the gnomes call Gilacia. In fact, there are many lands and different races of people and creatures that inhabit the Gilacia way below Holly Mills."

Piper's bewildered scowl was understandable. "So you're saying that under our town and all of South Jersey there's another land—another place where people are living right now?"

Nina winced. "Ah, yeah. That's right."

"You've got to be kidding me," Piper huffed.

"And not just our town and state, but way beyond it. And not only are there people down below, but fantastic creatures that you couldn't even imagine."

"How do you know all this? Who told you?" Piper asked with growing impatience overshadowed by doubt.

"Remember a year ago February when that weird thing happened and things that were moving away didn't look like they were moving away? Remember all the excitement on the television stations in Philly? Well, that was the day when I was standing right near this oak; I was shaking because I was so scared. Then the strangest thing happened. That hatch opened, and there he was staring out at me."

"Who was staring at you? What do you mean?"

"A gnome was gawking at me. After we introduced ourselves to one another, I discovered that he was very charming and friendly. He invited me inside the tree, explaining that he lived in the First Kingdom of the Gnomes far below our county and the other surrounding counties of the South Jersey. Oh, he was so nice, and we became great friends over many months."

"Better than you and me, I suppose?" snapped Piper.

"It's not like that. You are still my best friend," insisted Nina.

"But how can I…"

"Just listen! He took me down the yueblion, these stairs, on several occasions. I actually saw a part of the kingdom and witnessed an actual war. And, well, there's just too much to tell you as to what all happened."

"Gnomes, kingdoms? What's the matter with you? And what is this made-up stuff about a yuebli whatever?"

"Piper, you have to believe I'm telling you the truth."

Piper's stern appearance crumbled into a smirk. "Is this some stupid April Fool's joke or something? Come on, how do you really expect me to believe all that malarkey about an underground world?"

"I can see that you won't believe me unless you see for yourself." Nina jumped up and headed to the protruding piece of bark. She grabbed the knob and gave it a jerk and a twist. The side gave way as the small door flung outward, revealing darkness within. "Well, come see for yourself, Doubting Thomas!"

Piper stood up and inched her way to the enormous trunk. Nina slipped inside. "Come on, scaredy cat. Grab my hand."

Ducking her head, Piper moved into the dark room. Nina reached up to a bracket, grabbed the luminar, and lifted it out. Flipping the switch, they watched the object begin to glow. Nina shut the door while the luminar's light flooded the damp space. Moving the light toward the stairway, she turned to Piper with a wonderful smile.

"See this railing and the stairway spinning down into the darkness below? This is called a yueblion. Many yueblions were made centuries ago by some ancient people who built these to explore the uplands."

"The what?" Piper looked queasy.

"The uplands, the surface land where we all live. Now just stay here for a second."

Nina held the luminar in front of her and climbed downward about thirty feet. Piper watched in horror as her friend's petite figure diminished and darkness overwhelmed the trunk's interior.

"Piper, can you see me from up there? All I can see is darkness both upwards and downwards."

"Please come back now! I'm getting really nervous, Nina! Come back now!"

Nina scrambled back up the steps. Out of breath and panting, she hugged her quaking friend, whose head was swimming.

"I'm so sorry, Piper. I guess I'm so used to being in here and down below that I forgot what all this must be like for you."

"Let's get out of here because I'm getting the creeps," said Piper with a whimper.

Nina grabbed her by the shoulder and looked into her eye. "Piper Rae Slack, this is a shock for you. I realize that. But there's so much more. And I need your help. The gnomes need our help."

"If you think I'm going down there into the darkness and getting lost in some deep cave, you are whacko."

"You must trust me. Piper, we're best friends, and I've never lied to you or hurt you. Now I'm asking for your trust – to keep this a top secret and help me with a big problem."

Piper wiped the tears from her cheeks and looked into Nina's big hazel eyes. "Well, I'm not sure I can trust you since you never trusted me with your secrets. This is all so much to take in. I mean, it changes everything on how I think about things—and, well maybe even about our friendship."

"I know! Believe me, when I first met Edip, I was flabbergasted and scared out of my wits."

"You, scared? I find that hard to believe. And just how in the world you were able to keep all of this a secret from me, I'll never know."

"Piper, it was really hard, but I promised Edip to keep it a secret, even from you. Now let's leave; I'll tell you more later."

"Leaving is the best thing I've heard so far," said Piper as she turned toward the hatch.

Nina grasped the inner knob and cracked the hatchway. The invading sunlight pierced the darkness, nearly blinding the two girls.

"Wait a moment till our eyes get used to the daylight. Plus, I have to be on the lookout for anyone spying us leaving the tree trunk," whispered Nina, as if encroachers were close at hand.

The two paused, staring out at the lawn and hedge with squinting eyes. Suddenly, a shuffling sound broke the silence from behind. Piper spun around and gasped. Nina turned with the luminar still in her hand. The beams of light exposed the red conical cap and broad, wrinkled face of the astonished underlander peering up through the yueblion's cool railing.

Chapter Five

Reluctant Rescuer

Sunday, April 18 (morning)

T he stairs leading to the chancel were filled with white Easter lilies. Nina tried to count them during the sermon, but their array made it impossible to do so from her pew. She did not hear much of the message on the empty tomb. Instead, she pondered the extraordinary meeting that was to take place that afternoon.

Yesterday's encounter with Edip and Piper in the old oak was brief and awkward. Piper was mesmerized by the gnome's accent, mannerisms, and his very existence for that matter. Nina quietly giggled when she recalled how Piper stared at Edip as he stumbled to explain some of the secrets. Nina was hopeful that today's gathering would prove more fruitful for both her disconnected friends and the idea behind the rescue effort.

As promised, punctual Piper arrived at the Fithians' home at two o'clock. Minor chatter accompanied the girls to the backyard boundary and under the massive shade of the ancient tree. Nina stopped in her tracks and swung Piper around by her shoulders. They gazed eye-to-eye. Secrecy shrouded the two girls as they immersed themselves in the moment of imminent mystery.

"Piper, I apologize for not telling you more when we left Edip and the tree yesterday. It's just that I felt you couldn't take in any more."

Piper nodded. "I hate to admit it, but you're right. I felt like a balloon with too much air in it—ready to pop. Then again, I must say it's great that you finally 'fessed up about these secrets you've been keeping from me. After all, we're not supposed to hold things from each other."

"Now, Piper Rae, I really don't want to go through all that. We have more important things to do right now. Remember I told you about the gnomes needing our help?"

Piper shook her head halfheartedly, as if torn between wanting to know more and remaining happily ignorant.

"Well, Edip came to me last Friday night while I was in my room. He told me there's a crisis in the kingdom. Princess Cirlaena has been kidnapped and taken to a faraway land down below. Some evil lord in Castle Darken-something is holding her prisoner."

"But why?" asked Piper.

"I'm not sure."

"Is she being held for ransom?"

"Again, I don't really know. Actually, I forget a lot of the details about the whole thing, but I do know we're being asked to help in her rescue."

Piper lowered her brows, expressing volumes before she even spoke. "How in the blue blazes are two girls supposed to help in some underground rescue, and in the dark? Are you off your rocker? What about our parents and the trip tomorrow? And how are we going to explain leaving to Mrs. Gaskell? Plus, did I forget to tell you that all this scares the beegeebers out of me? We could get killed!"

"I understand how you feel more than you think. But Edip promised me that we will not be harmed and that he'll take care of us."

"But why us?" Piper whined.

Nina wrung her hands in frustration. "There's this wise one, a Grand Patriarch named Feedunkulus. This old gnome can kinda see into the future. He knows all things. All the gnomes really respect his advice and opinions. He claims that a Kimonos is the only way to get their princess safely back to the kingdom."

"Wait. What's a kamonis? I suppose it means something in gnome language, right?"

Nina laughed. "Yes, silly! It's a special team – in this case made up of five people: Edip, another gnome, a starling, and you and me."

"A starling? What in the world is that?"

"He's a creature from the underlands who lives toward Atlantic City and north under the seashore. I haven't met one up close – only from afar during the war last year."

"What war?"

"The war last year down below," said Nina.

"Huh! Now I'm really confused – even more than before."

"Look it, forget the war already."

"But I wanna know—"

"Piper, just give Edip a chance to meet with us and give us the lowdown, all right?"

It was nearly time for the rendezvous. Nina waited patiently beside the great trunk as Piper paced from side to side. Finally, the hatchway opened with the squinting gnome hidden among the shadows, careful not to reveal himself to anyone but the girls.

"Come inside. Hurry – bring your friend too," Edip said quietly.

With an assuring grip, Nina held Piper's hand and they entered the dark enclosure. Even with the glowing luminar mounted on the wall, they could barely make out his diminutive form when the hatch shut.

"Thank you both for meeting with me. Piper, it is a pleasure to see you again. Sorry to have startled you yesterday."

"Oh, that's all right. I do frighten easily. Just ask Nina. She could write a book on that." Nina put her arm around her friend and giggled. Edip smiled and reached out to shake Piper's hand. Piper reciprocated, thinking how strange it was to touch the coarse, wrinkled skin of a foreign creature.

"I see you are somewhat perplexed by me. Do not be afraid. You and I are destined to become good friends, right Nina?" said the good-natured gnome.

"Of course, Edip," said Nina. "Piper will grow to love you as I do. Piper, he's the best. Wait and see!"

Faint taps became more pronounced as a spinning conical cap rose from the yueblion. Each step upward revealed more of another stout figure. By now the girls' vision was quite accustomed to the dim light.

"Nina Fithian and Piper Slack, allow me to introduce you to the revered gnomen warrior, General Rozen Shäbáhn."

The decorated officer bowed gracefully then stood erect with pride and determination. His ornate uniform bespoke of military importance. His expression bordered on being severely troubled. Tucked under his right arm was a parchment portfolio stuffed with documents and maps.

After catching his breath, the general spoke. "It is a pleasure to meet you, girls. Before I ask you both to join our quest, may I take just a few moments to explain the dark and dire circumstances that have led our paths to this very place?"

Piper looked at Nina's large eyes, which were fixed on the general, and then followed suit. She studied the medals and ribbons on his jacket and was amused by the gnome's unusual brogue. His loud throat-clearing brought her attention back to what he was saying.

Shäbáhn explained about the abduction of Cirlaena by Lord Borok and provided vague but plausible reasons as to why it had occurred.

"We suspect the trollian government has a hand in this deed. Emperor Shaptillicus swore vengeance on our king and kingdom after his defeat in the last war. It stands to reason that the kidnapping is a plot to overthrow the throne and cast the First Kingdom into total disarray. Nonetheless, the Kimonos is our only hope to rescue Princess Cirlaena."

Shäbáhn stepped forward, taking each girl by the hand. "Nina, Piper, I know we have no claim of loyalty upon you, but we beseech you both to join us in this noble cause."

"Do we stand a good chance of succeeding?" asked Nina.

"Are we going to get hurt or harmed? Will you protect us?" blurted Piper.

"I cannot assure you of anything except we will do our very best to protect you and keep you safe. I can promise you the greatest adventure of your life filled with memories to last a lifetime! And I can tell you that if we do not rescue the princess soon she will surely die."

A wave of sadness flooded the small interior.

"Die? Why would she die?" said Nina.

"I have spoken too much," said the general, whose solemn gaze lowered to the wooden ground. "Will you join us? Will you unite with the Kimonos to rescue fair Cirlaena, our beloved heir to the throne?"

Silence draped the four as Shäbáhn's words faded in an echo that cascaded down the spiraling yueblion. Nina turned to Piper. A sentimental sensation hovered about them like finches too fearful to perch and too weary to fly away.

"Piper, I'll do it, but only if we do it together. We've been through so many adventures: the tornado monster, the haunted house, the mirage man, the night shadows, alien lights. So what's one more great mystery or adventure?"

"One more? You talk like this is some walk in the park! We're talking about taking a journey to places we've never been before with strange things that may hurt us."

"True, but we will have our gnome friends by our side, that starling scout, and each other," Nina said as she broke into a convincing grin.

"So, if we don't go and help, then the princess might die?" asked Piper.

Nina gave Piper one of her puppy dog expressions.

"Oh, you!" Piper grumbled. "If I say *no*, I'll never hear the end of it."

Nina hugged her best friend. Edip smiled, but the general's countenance remained serious.

"Piper, Nina, I will come to your house tomorrow after your families leave for the trip. Make sure you pack clothing for at least four days. I will take care of the rest," said Edip.

The girls bid their goodbyes and exited into the brightness, closing the hatch behind them. The sunshine made it difficult to walk back to the house.

Still within the trunk, the two gnomes faced one another with questioning expressions.

Edip spoke first. "Well, general, what are your thoughts?"

"Much is riding on such youthful courage and utter inexperience. But I have to believe that Feedunkulus has made the correct and wise choice. They seem to possess inner qualities that can guide the rescue."

"I agree."

"And you are right, my friend. They do look so much alike – and so energetic and sweet."

"That much is certain," quipped Edip.

The general nodded. "Yes, but I worry about Piper. She may become a liability along the way."

"Ah, but Nina will uphold her in times of trouble. Valor will be drawn from their devotion to one another," said Edip.

"I trust that is the case, my dear old friend. I hope so for the sake of Cirlaena and our beloved kingdom. The princess must return to the waters soon. The promise of Zandra demands it."

Chapter Six

Perfect Alibi

Monday, April 19 (morning)

The commotion about the Fithian home was evidenced by murmuring and bustling as Edward and Barbara Fithian put the final touches on packing for the trip to Boston. Nina Leigh sat on the stairs petting Bailey and watching Dad carry the suitcases toward the door leading to the garage. Her mom frantically searched for the maps and traveler's checks.

In some respects Nina wished that she and Piper were going along with their parents.

The two-toned chime of the doorbell interrupted the scurrying. In walked the frumpy and rotund Mrs. Gaskell, the aged babysitter. She gave token hugs and kisses to all and nestled her suitcase and shopping bags by the staircase. She turned to greet Nina when the doorbell sounded again, signaling the renowned punctuality of Dr. Slack. While the parents greeted each other, Piper dropped her backpack and darted to her friend. Turning to the two young brunettes, Mrs. Gaskell offered salutations, which tumbled vainly into the air as the girls flew up the stairs to Nina's room.

Behind closed door, the would-be twins held hands and giggled like two youngsters about to enter a carnival for the first time.

Piper spoke first. "Has Edip been here yet to help us with the getaway plan? What's he got up his sleeve?"

Nina ran her fingers through her long wavy locks and sported a curious grin. "All I know is he's bringing something that will allow us to spend lots of time away from here without being noticed. Knowing that clever old gnome like I do, I bet he's spying on our house this very moment, waiting to come in once our parents leave."

"Nina, I hate to say it, but I'm getting excited about this whole rescue thing. And I must admit that without you in my life things would be rather boring."

Nina snickered and performed an arabesque to show off her dancing talents. "Not to brag, but I am quite a catch as a best friend."

"Now let's not get too haughty," said Piper with a spirited laugh.

Mrs. Fithian's voice called up the stairwell. "Nina, Piper, we're leaving soon. Come on down so we can say goodbye."

The girls skipped down the staircase and hugged their parents. Lance had already walked to the car to see Mrs.

Slack, who was holding Piper's baby sister, Laura Lynn. Within minutes the hubbub settled, save for a few whimpers from Bailey, whose incessant howls sent Mrs. Gaskell into the other room.

Nina and Piper climbed back upstairs and buried themselves in Nina's bedroom with a host of thoughts for what was ahead. Suddenly they heard a rap on the window. Nina gaited to the glass to steal a look onto the lawn. The hiding gnome was hurling acorns up at the window to gain their attention. Signaling to her bearded friend, Nina turned to Piper with exclamation.

"Piper, he's down there! Quick, come with me." Nina grabbed her friend, who was a smidgen taller, and nearly stumbled down the stairs in excitement.

"Girls, please refrain from horseplay in the house. You both know how it makes me nervous and gets Bailey barking."

"Sorry, Mrs. Gaskell. We'll be in the backyard on the swings," replied Nina.

With that, they sprang into the garage and out the side service door. Shooting around the house and across the thick, grassy lawn, they discreetly approached Edip, who was concealed behind the tall hedge near the giant oak.

"It's great to see you again," said Nina, panting, with Piper staring over her shoulder.

"Likewise, girls." With that he reached into the big pocket of his baggy trousers and pulled out a small device that resembled a silver portable radio with a curly aerial attached on top.

"I'm assuming that the nanny is within and the adults have departed on their trip, correct?" asked the little man.

"Yes, we're home alone with Mrs. Gaskell. I think she's inside watching soap operas," offered Nina.

"Excellent! Now, girls, this will provide for both of you the perfect alibi to come to the underlands for many days.

This small box I hold within my hands is a transitronic deceleron. I will activate it as such."

He flipped an orange switch on its side that caused the small dials to glow with brilliance. The girls stared at the mechanism in wonder and caution.

"What on earth does it do?" asked Piper with a slight stutter.

"It is a marvel for sure. The device was made decades ago by the mêdebáhn, for they wanted a means in which to explore the uplands without human interruption or detection. The elfin government had entrusted this unit to our king, for scientific purposes of course.

"You see, it alters the fourth dimension to any speed that you set by the red knob. The green knob adjusts the spatial effect. In other words, the deceleron can slow time in just your home so that Mrs. Gaskell thinks an hour has passed when in fact days have transpired. Now, are you both packed for the journey as I instructed you?"

"Yes, our backpacks are stuffed for the trip. We're quite ready," Nina remarked.

"Good. Now it's time to commence the adventure. I will show you what to do." With those words as an overture, he detailed what they needed to know and where to plant the device.

Nina and Piper hurried to the garage and entered, heading straightaway to the foyer. Opening the closet doors, Nina pushed the gloves and scarves aside on the shelf and set the mechanism down. She turned the dials and knobs to the proper calibration. For a moment she paused, staring at the round start button. Just one push would throw everything into motion. And it did.

A shimmering noise filled the hallway and foyer as she slid the closet door shut. A wave of motion sickness overcame them. Quickly they grabbed their gear and stole a peek at Mrs. Gaskell, who was still reclined in the family room chair. Nodding to each other, the girls rushed out to meet the gnome.

"Watch the house," said Edip. The girls turned toward the structure to see it glow for a fraction of a second, then return to normal. "See that blotch over the house that resembles a small, cloudy mirage? Well, that is a sign that the device is actuated."

Piper looked worried. "Will anyone notice it, Edip?"

"Heavens no. We are the only ones who can see the effect."

The girls were too dumbstruck to respond. They just stood with their mouths opened in astonishment.

"Come now. We have miles to go and a princess to rescue." Edip hurried toward the trunk and opened the hatch. The girls followed close behind, disappearing into the dark interior.

The mounted luminar did not help the girls' vision adjust much to the dimness, and Edip knew it. Therefore, he engaged them in small conversation until their eyes acclimated to the darkened enclosure. Minutes later, he reached into his baggy pockets and withdrew three other small bronze cylinders.

"Here's one for each of us," he said.

"What are they?" asked Piper.

Edip smiled and handed her a lighting instrument. "Piper, this is a luminar, invented by the elves centuries ago. They operate through a special chemical process."

"Wow, this is so neat!" said Piper, studying its unique design.

He cleared his throat. "As you know, we have a ways to go. Piper, stay close to Nina and fear not. You are perfectly safe with us."

"And, Piper, I want to warn you – going down the yueblion will make you a little lightheaded and tired," offered Nina.

"I'll be okay – I think?"

51

The gnome moved toward the yueblion and held the cool, semicircular railing. "Here we go!"

With one step he began the long, lonely descent. Nina held Piper's hand as they moved down into the well. Piper's heart thumped with each stride into the unknown. Her eyes darted to and fro at the rocky walls that encased the twisting stone and metal stairway, but the fear of stumbling kept her attention to the ancient steps.

Spiraling down and down, the intrepid trio entered the first leg of their arduous mission – one that would reveal more about themselves than the unexpected that awaited them below like a haunting specter.

Chapter Seven

Battle and the Bailiwicks

Monday, April 19 (midday)

The gnome led them down the dark yueblion. Each carried a luminar, but the light was of no comfort to the newcomer, who was very anxious over being in the huge vertical shaft. Piper's racing heartbeat had subsided. She gripped the cool metal railing that wove along the spiraling stone slabs. Positioned between Edip and Nina, she watched each step while her imagination ran wild with speculations of mishaps along the way. Her mind envisioned falling rocks, flying bats, creeping spiders, and anything else that could be scary, harmful, or deadly. The chilled air became thicker; her breathing was labored. Piper knew herself far too well and realized that if she did not get her thoughts on something else, she would surely faint.

"Nina, Edip," she huffed, breaking the silence, "tell me about this war you keep talking about."

"Are you sure you wanna know?" asked Nina.

"Yes, might as well know about it since we are going to where it all happened."

Nina rolled her eyes and shook her head. "Okay, let's see, where do I begin? And, Edip, help me out if I forget something."

"Glad to oblige," said the leader.

"Well, it was nearly a year ago – yes, last May around Memorial Day. I remember lying in the hammock reading a book when suddenly I was nearly thrown to the ground by some kind of weird lightning storm. All at once I felt dizzy, sick to my stomach. Piper, remember all the commotion on the news warning people about some kind of unusual weather effect in the Delaware Valley?"

"Yeah, I remember people living by the shore being afraid of some kind of cyclone or something like that."

Nina continued. "Well, after watching the news with my mother, I ran out to the tree, hoping that Edip would show up. I thought he might know what was going on."

"Was he there?" asked Piper.

"No," Nina said sheepishly.

"Well, what did you do? What happened next? And what's this got to do with a war?"

"Be patient. Gosh! Anyway, I decided to enter the trunk and go down to find Edip."

"Down the yueblion by yourself? Alone?" Piper was aghast.

Edip chuckled. "Yes she did, against my standing advice, of course. Luckily she knew the way to our land fairly well."

Nina's speech became more rapid. "Look it, I went all the way down the yueblion and into the caverns and all. Finally at the end of the tunnels, I got to the big chamber that opens to the kingdom. I hurried down the ramp and hightailed it all the way to Edip's house."

The gnome interrupted. "Then, Piper, our curious friend told me about all the confusion that happened in the uplands."

"And remember how upset you were, Edip?" Nina said.

"Were you upset with Nina?" Piper asked.

They stopped where the yueblion widened. Benches hewn into the jagged wall offered them rest.

Rubbing his knees, Edip sighed. "No, I was not upset with Nina – surprised to see her, but not upset. What disturbed me was the thought of invasion. Who could forget that fateful day?"

Turning to Piper, Nina said, "Piper, it was awful. I was in the middle of explaining the electric-wave thing to Edip when all of a sudden there was an explosion from far away."

"Actually, it was artillery fire from the Western Barrion, from the trollian forces," explained the gnome.

Nina told Piper how the gnomes hurried through the streets like ants and of the ominous feeling that something horrible was about to unfold. She paused to tie her shoelaces.

"What happened?" Piper said, shaking Nina's shoulder.

"Gosh – hold on! The next thing I remember was Edip grabbing my arm and telling me to follow him. We both dashed down the main street, which led to this tall statue at the center of the city. Thousands, and I mean thousands, of gnomes were gathering. Many were already dressed in army uniforms. It was quite a sight – yelling and hollering, like no one was listening to each other until the viceroy stood on the steps of the statue. What exactly did he say, Edip? I can't remember that part."

Edip stood facing the girls. "It was a stirring address, a call to arms if you will. Viceroy Ober reminded the gnomes of our beloved war hero, Vahit, whose brilliant strategies and valor brought victory to our kingdom. You see, girls, long ago his leadership kept our lands safe and secure from our enemies. These same virtues were what the viceroy spoke of to meet the grave challenges that we faced back then. The viceroy also explained how our Gnomen Federate Army was already engaged in skirmishes with the trolls at the Duruflaé Schism in the west."

"But I thought your country was surrounded by these huge rock walls," said Piper.

"This is true, but the barrions have passes, and it is those very tunnels that make our people vulnerable to attack."

Edip signaled the girls to continue their descent. A few minutes later he resumed his recollections, describing how the gnomen forces were partially successful in containing the enemy's forward advances. He also mentioned that special envoys had been sent to the Elfin Realm and Starling Sphere, with hopes that these allied governments would render aid.

"Edip, tell Piper more about these enemies," insisted Nina.

"Ah, yes. Our archenemy, Shaptillicus, is ruler of the Trollian Empire. He is very powerful and in league with the weak-minded goblin king, Orgetarex. Shaptillicus is also an ally to Areovistus, the gozzi leader in the northwest.

"Last year our spies learned that Shaptillicus planned to penetrate the Duruflaé Schism, while the goblins and the gozzi had orders to invade from Docapishu Pass in the north."

"But how could you have won against so many?" asked Piper.

"We knew that if our allies did not arrive on time, we would have been overtaken."

"The machine! Tell Piper about the foto-thing!"

No one spoke for a few seconds. Only the echo of their footsteps could be heard.

Edip broke the silence. "Piper, the trolls also had planned to use a secret doomsday weapon they had stolen from another evil race. Our spies learned that it was a Focused Temporal Accelerator. You see, when aimed at anything, the FOTAR machine sends out a bright beam of warped energy, creating a time-rush effect. The mechanism destroys everything in its path and would allow the trolls to besiege one borough after another. The strange effect that Nina had described in the uplands was nothing more than the trolls testing the machine through the upper rock layers."

So intrigued with the story was she that Piper tripped into the gnome, who was able to steady her.

"Sorry, Edip, but please tell me what happened next," pleaded Piper.

"My first thoughts were to get Nina to safety," replied Edip.

The gnome described how he and Nina had run to the south and climbed to the ledge near the opening of the dark chamber. Once there both witnessed the onset of war from afar. Edip reached into his deep pocket and withdrew a pair of high-powered binoculars. Briefly he looked through them and then handed them to Nina.

From the Southern Barrion she witnessed the rancorous points of battle. Far north at the Hala Shala Outpost gnomen troops were defending the Docapishu Pass. To the west at the Gen-Gann Guly Outpost the Gnomen Federate Army was defending the breach in the Duruflaé Schism. All gnomes knew that if Gen-Gann fell, the Western Frontier of Krenari and the borough of Mosma Cha-Calkin would become the front line of trollian engagement.

Sharing the binoculars, Nina and Edip had sadly watched the battlefields. The crack and crash of guns and cannonfire echoed off the great rocky palisades. Nina covered her ears from the deafening sounds of this strange, subterranean warfare. Invasion was imminent.

"But the gnomes won, didn't they?" Piper said.

"Let him finish," insisted Nina.

"All was just about lost when suddenly there was a magnificent crack followed by a thunderous explosion from the Eastern Barrion. A whistling sound rocketed across the smoky sky. A second explosion, much louder than the first, was heard in the west. Later I learned that the FOTAR weapon was destroyed by the starlings' cannon."

"Was that it? Was the war over?" asked Piper.

"No, but it was the beginning of the end – for the enemy. You see, as soon as the machine was blown to bits, thousands of ropes dropped from the sky in the west. Elves and starling commandoes slid downward and raced into the conflict. Within minutes the tide of the battle turned. The forward onslaught of the enemy had been halted near both passes. An hour later the gnomes and their brave allies had driven the enemy into retreat."

"So did Shaptillicus finally surrender?" Piper asked.

The gnome did not speak until he came to another resting platform. Stopping, he turned to the girls. "The emperor will never give up. He wants what we possess – that which was promised to my people long, long ago. No, Shaptillicus retreated with his minions and allies to fight on another day."

Piper cocked her head. "But you said that the kandalarians have kidnapped the princess. Why them and not the trolls?"

Edip shook his head and looked down, his expression troubled. "The kandalarians are being used by the trolls. They are puppets of Shaptillicus. The Grand Patriarch has surmised that the trolls have plotted to start another war with us – indirectly and internally. And this is where the kidnapping fits in. Shaptillicus knows that if the princess dies, confusion and despair will envelop the kingdom. It is then at our weakest hour that his forces will most likely strike!"

But the gnome's words were not entirely true, for not even the wisest of the little people could perceive the true nature and depth of the enemy's diabolical plan.

Chapter Eight

King and the Kimonos

Monday, April 19 (afternoon)

Piper wielded the glowing bronze luminar with her out-stretched hand, studying the walls of the small cavern at the yueblion's base. The dank, cool air wrapped around her frame like a blanket, reducing the dizzying effect of the long descent. Her mouth hung open in amazement. Nina kept staring at her best friend's expression with amusement.

Edip led the girls into an adjoining chamber studded with rich crystals on the domed ceiling. The exquisite jewels sparkled with color. Piper scanned every part of the massive room. Just beyond the chamber Edip escorted them through a long, winding tunnel that grew darker at each bend. Piper knew for sure that, left by herself, she would be utterly lost.

Finally the three travelers arrived at another mammoth chamber, which had a great cleft on its opposite side.

"Piper, you've got to see this. You won't believe your eyes," exclaimed Nina with an urgency that could only be measured by the pressure of her grip. Nina pulled the bewildered newcomer toward the large opening in the rock.

Once beyond the cleft, the three stood on a wide ledge that provided a vista of the vast alien land. Piper's gasps of wonder made Nina giggle with delight. Piper scanned the breadth of the huge valley below and beyond, all surrounded by the massive barrions—the rocky crags, precipices, and bluffs that encircled the kingdom like an impregnable mountain range.

"Piper Rae, was this worth the wait or what?" said Nina.

The gnome stepped forward with one arm around Piper's shoulder and the other outstretched ahead. "Piper Slack, behold the First Kingdom."

Piper's eyes were drawn to the sparse, scattered forests and strange vegetation intermingled with tall teal-colored tamarack trees. A winding river zigzagged through the land from south to north with a lake located toward the middle of the river's length and the kingdom's lands.

"Edip, tell her about the boroughs, the hamlets, the capital, and the passes," harped Nina.

Still pointing ahead, he quickly explained, "Up ahead of us is the hamlet of Maraffta Peka, and just beyond is the borough of Pro-coak Toanday where our Grand Patriarch lives. See the towers far in the distance? That is our capital, Gnomen City, where the king and queen reside in the Royal Palace. Next to it is Spoleo Hall, our seat of government.

"Now to the far north are the borough of Spirtee Teim and the hamlets of Shopkah and Fahto. To the east are the great passes leading to our allies—starlings, elves, and the ipoli.

"And now to the northwest in the far horizon, way beyond the capital, is Dabuffta Nunu, and north of that borough is the Docapishu Pass, which is guarded by garrisons."

"Wasn't Dabuffta Nunu named after the gozzi invasion of the borough?" asked Nina.

"Yes," said Edip. "The name means 'city that rebuffed the beasts.' You see, many years ago the gozzi-nunu forces invaded from the north and captured the small settlement. In a fierce battle, our army was able to drive the gozzi back through the Docapishu Pass. That is why our troops are always stationed at the mouth of the northern and western passes to prevent invasion from our enemies."

"Wow! The gnomes have lots of enemies," said Piper.

"Yep, there are plenty of evil creatures that would just as soon see all the gnomes destroyed," replied Nina.

"Nina is correct. The gozzi and goblins are a constant threat, even after the last war a year ago. This leads me to Mosma Cha-Calkin, the great borough in the Western Frontier of Krenari. Although you can't see it, it is a thriving yet anxious community since it is poised so close to the Duruflaé Schism."

Piper cocked her head. "Where's that? I'm lost."

"Like I told you on the way down, the Duruflaé Schism is a massive break in the Western Barrion. The opening is always guarded by our troops. They always watch for more clever and insidious foe – the wicked trolls, who are all under the devious domination of their emperor. Remember that in the last war Shaptillicus was successful in uniting

many of our enemies against us. It is he and his trollian minions whom we believe are behind the abduction of Princess
Cirlaena."

With that he motioned to the girls to follow him down the
rocky ramp, which descended to an obscure pathway. Along
the way Piper filled their ears with question after question
about the land and gnomen culture.

"Edip, it's almost like dawn or dusk down here. Looking
up at the rock ceiling way up there, I can't see where the
light's coming from," Piper said, continuing with the
inquisition.

"That, Young One, is what we refer to as the gloaming.
It is illumination emanating from the very rocks above us."

"But how do the rocks make the light?"

"From what we understand, it is a combination of chrys-
olampis stone and white phosphorous bands. Without these
deposits embedded in the great dome above us, the valley
would be uninhabitable."

As they passed through Maraffta Peka and by Pro-coak
Toanday, their steady conversation was redirected back to
the trolls and their utter contempt for the First Kingdom.

"Why do they hate you all so much?" asked Piper.

The gnome sighed. "Piper, sometimes hate runs so deep
that the hater is unable to distinguish between the root of the
hatred and that which drives it onward. Look way ahead to
the spires. There is Gnomen City."

Edip quickened his pace with the girls following suit.
They weaved through the outskirts and proceeded straight
for Spoleo Hall. A beautiful outer walkway adorned with
colonnades connected Spoleo to the Royal Palace.

"Before we enter Spoleo Hall, turn your eyes to the left
and behold its beauty," Edip said with an outstretched arm.

Piper and Nina turned and gasped in delight at the
splendor of the riverside community.

Edip continued. "Yes, behold the mighty Zander Zee River—resplendent and magnificent. See how it gently meanders into crystalline Lake Tangelee."

"I have never seen anything so beautiful before. It's glorious!" said Piper, her eyes fixed on the shimmering waters.

"Piper, there's so much beauty down here. Wait till you see the other boroughs," said Nina with a gleam in her eyes.

The gnome guided them into the pristine hall filled with opulence and grandeur. Led through a huge set of golden doors, the girls anticipated a gathering of high-ranking officials. Their hopes were not disappointed. In the center of the large, decorated room was an immense gopherwood table surrounded by tall brass chairs. Seated about the great oval were dignitaries, military officials, and the king himself. Nina recognized some of the twenty members, including Generals Shäbáhn and Dalandúshae, Gnomen City Mayor Stout, Viceroy Ober, and Feedunkulus, the Grand Patriarch.

His Majesty rose, followed by his entourage. "Enter and be seated, my welcomed guests. Our servants will provide for you a meal while we talk about the mission. General Shäbáhn, please carry on with the agenda."

The general stood and straightened his official, ribbon-studded jacket while the servants presented the sumptuous treats and guato juice to the three sojourners.

Looking at Edip, the general said, "I assume the alibi has been established for the girls and that all has transpired according to our plan."

Edip nodded. "Yes, general. Everything is according to the plan."

"Excellent! As I have foreseen," said the great Feedunkulus.

"Yes, excellent," confirmed Shäbáhn. "Now our focus is on the mission to rescue the princess. We have no more than four days to return her to the kingdom. Otherwise, Her Majesty will surely die and we will be at war once again."

The words of the general sent chills down the spines of the two friends.

Shäbáhn continued. "After the dawning the Kimonos will rendezvous at SheeNao Depot at 0730 hours to ready for the journey. The starling scout will meet you at the depot and accompany you on the mission. He will be in charge of navigating the lands; Edip will lead the Kimonos. Provisions and equipment have been packed."

"General, for the sake of our friends from the uplands, would you please elaborate on the journey, including the challenges that the Kimonos will encounter?" asked Edip.

"But of course. In the morn the Kimonos will travel south from Gnomen City along the Zander Zee. At KaylaLind Gardens, you will cross over the bridge and pass through the hamlet of Posha. Heading southwest, you will traverse through the eastern border of the Wilderness of Meriami until you get to the Southern Barrion. Edip will show you the secret pass through the rock that provides access into Bedloe Abidion. There you will face trials of the mind.

"Once past that land you will enter Creetswarron, where you may come face-to-face with the swamp creature."

"Excuse me, but what's that?" asked a worried Piper.

Shäbáhn explained. "It's a test of your courage; fear not! Your guides will know what to do. From Creetswarron you will proceed to Tremória. From our rough calculations, you must pass through the rocks in intervals of thirties. However, we trust that the scout will be able to discern this more fully."

"General, the starlings are confident that Tremória will not be a problem for the Kimonos," offered Enver, the second gnome and good friend of Edip who would take part in the Kimonos. Nina discerned a touch of doubt in his voice.

"Let us hope so, my brave friend. From the quaking zone you will journey through Ílda-dunn, which will bring you to the petrified glades. Once past the threat of the worms, you will approach the boundaries of Kandalar."

The general paused and took a sip of the sweet beverage from the tall crystal goblet. Nina stole a glance at Piper and saw the apprehension on her countenance. Under the table Nina gently squeezed Piper's hand to comfort her troubled friend. Their eyes met as Nina whispered, "We'll be all right—honest."

General Shäbáhn lowered the goblet and continued, curtailing Nina's comforting words. "Once in Kandalar the Kimonos will proceed with haste to Castle Darkondusk to find the princess. Once she is found and freed, you will backtrack, following a similar route back to the kingdom."

"That does not leave much time for the return journey," offered General Dalandúshae.

Shäbáhn looked around the table and continued. "I can surmise by your expressions you fear that success is rather dubious. However, I assure you that the starling has many tricks up his silken sleeves, so to speak. He is both wise and bold. Trust his instincts and rely upon his sound judgment."

"Thank you, General Shäbáhn. And now let us feast and fellowship," encouraged the king with a meager smile.

During the meal plans were discussed about lodging for the night and the morning meeting. Nina and Piper chattered between themselves and launched questions across to Edip and Enver. Although the food was delicious, the girls were transfixed on elements of the rescue and the great unknowns.

"Are you worried, Nina? I mean, do you think we're up to this?" whispered Piper.

"To be honest, I'm a little nervous, but I trust Edip and these gnomes. I believe in them. I believe in the rescue. And through it we are going to experience such wonderful things that we would've never know unless we took part in the journey."

Piper's eyebrows lifted in an ambivalent expression. Nina leaned over and gave her a sisterly embrace.

Chapter Nine

Two Confessions

Tuesday, April 20 (morning)

A fter breakfast the girls stood outside of the gothic-style structure. The bustling crowds entering and exiting SheeNao Depot could mesmerize any bystander. Nina and Piper were riveted to the potpourri of gnomish characters flitting about with their provincial business, totally unaware of the mission. Only the obvious, curious stares of the passersby made the moment uncomfortable for the girls as they stood by Edip and Enver.

General Shäbáhn came around the corner of the colonnade walkway with a leather portfolio and signaled the four to follow him past the guarded doorway. Once inside the great room, Shäbáhn approached the center table where he spread out his maps and documents.

"The special boden backpacks by the bookshelf contain the supplies you will need. Take your belongings and place them inside the packs. Do not worry. There is enough room within the packs to contain your personals," said Shäbáhn with a stern imperative.

The four followed his directions and stuffed the cloth packs accordingly. The general motioned that they should all take a seat around the brass-and-glass rectangular table. Suddenly the door swung open. A tall figure stood erect, panting as if he had just been running. His deep-set eyes scanned the room with a stoic glare. His dark fine hair was combed downward over his forehead. The long green trenchcoat he wore was unseasonable and baggy, covering his lanky frame like Spanish moss on a Floridian pine. Camouflaged in plainness, his clothing denoted husbandry.

"Ah! You are just in time, my friend. Please be seated and join us," said Shäbáhn.

The solemn foreigner sat between the general and Enver and kept a steady gaze on the girls, giving them a discernible uneasiness.

"Now the Kimonos is complete. Nina, Piper, Edip, and Enver, I wish to introduce your mission scout and pathfinder. This is Hodges, a starling of the Häagen Clan."

The starling interrupted his steady stare with a monotone salutation. "I bring you greetings from the Northeast Lands. I must say, I was not expecting the Kimonos to be comprised of young human females."

"I assure you, Hodges, that this was ordained by the Grand Patriarch himself. You are all essential to the Kimonos and the success of the rescue effort," the general affirmed with a subtle twitch in his left eye.

"So be it. Who am I to question the wisdom of Feedunkulus?" The starling looked down at the stacked parchments and stroked his chiseled jaw.

"And now, my friends, please pay close attention to the map." Shäbáhn unfolded the document for reference. "You will begin your journey immediately, taking the southern route to the barrion."

Shäbáhn continued, detailing the first leg of the journey for the eager onlookers. After thirty minutes of briefing, they all stood. The team grabbed their effects and readied themselves for the long trek. The door opened; a starling adjutant entered with a dog-like creature tugging on a leash.

Shäbáhn grinned. "Ah yes, I nearly forgot. Hodges, please take along Yurggie. Remember how well he served us during Operation Gózgo? He will serve you equally on this daunting rescue."

The cannoid stood on its hinds. His attempts to steal a lick from Hodges' cheek was met with restrained affection.

"Yes, good to see you again, Yurggie. Now down to the ground!"

The general stepped forward, looking upon them as if to invoke a benediction. "And now Godspeed to you all, and may the promise of Zandra rest upon this Kimonos. And may the Lord of Hosts be your strength."

The time flew by while Nina and Piper chatted along the way. With no other means available, they traveled by the river, absorbed in conversation until Nina saw the highlands and vast wilderness of Meriami.

"My goodness! I don't remember much since we walked over the Kaylalind Bridge and through that small town or hamlet," announced Piper.

"Yeah, ever since we crossed over the Zander Zee, I haven't paid much attention to where we were going," said Nina.

"Girls, keep a look about for torial holes. They are more prevalent as we reach the foothills between the Wilderness of Meriami and the Southern Barrion," warned Edip.

"What are those holes you mentioned?" asked Piper.

"Little creatures in these parts burrow about, making small holes. Be careful or you could sprain an ankle tripping into one of them."

The girls continued their chatter, their eyes peering at the ridged, sandy soil. Suddenly a thought diverted Nina's attention.

"Piper Rae, remember back at the class party last Thursday? Remember when you said you saw someone hiding in the cloakroom?"

Piper raised her brow. "Well, like I already told you, I saw some girl with golden hair. She was wearing a white and blue dress, or maybe she had on an apron..."

Nina cut her short. "And wearing a white bonnet?"

"Yes. Good heavens, what difference does it make?"

"But I have to know exactly what—"

"Look it! You blurted out her name. You said *Aurora*. And, by the way, you still haven't given me a straight answer on that whole thing."

Nina's expression became more serious. "Actually, her name is Arianna, Arianna Angeliqué."

"Well, if you know who she is, then why wouldn't you tell me the whole story last week?"

Nina paused and took a deep breath. "Well, I didn't get a chance to. The bell rang, everyone was leaving, you left with your mom for your appointment, and..."

"Oh come on!" Piper said, exasperated. "You avoided me like the plague. You wouldn't even look at me when I left school that day. And when I called you, you either wouldn't pick up or, when I *did* get through, you conveniently changed the subject."

Nina slowed her brisk pace. "All right. I'll tell you this much. You did see someone, but she is supposed to be a secret. She is part of all the secrets."

"Oh great – something else you've kept from me," snapped Piper as she rolled her eyes.

"Like I told you, the girl's name is Arianna Angeliqué. She's a...a Wish-Weaver, a wonderful being from the Jêhvahaér race."

"What in the world is a Wish-Weaver?"

"Oh, this is really hard to explain. Well, you see, Arianna is part fairy godsister and part angel; at least I think that's true. To be honest I'm not sure what she truly is. Arianna's the one who granted me my wish about a year and a half ago."

"And the wish was?" she response with a snide tone

"Remember my eleventh birthday party? Well, I made a wish. It was no ordinary wish. My wish was to have the most unusual and weird adventures that anyone had ever had. Well, guess what? It all came true!"

"Huh?"

"Yep, it all started with my birthday cake. Remember how the cake changed, how all the girls saw the icing and candles in different colors?"

Piper nodded. "Yes, that was bizarre. Even your mom thought we were all playing a joke on her."

"Well, it was no joke – no trick. And shortly after that I met Arianna at the dress shop in Vinton. But at the time I didn't know who she was. Even then she had been watching me and planning all those bizarre times."

"You mean that..."

"Yes!" said Nina, gesturing with her hands. "And you were in some of those wild adventures too. Remember the living shadows in my bedroom? Remember the awful dream I had about the silver robot?"

"And I suppose the cloakroom getting larger during June Fete was part of it too?"

Nina nodded.

"And that night we saw those strange flying saucer lights near Oakland?"

Nina smiled. "Exactly! Remember our class elections when you arrived late to school and almost lost the election? Remember how the clock stopped, giving you time to win the votes?"

"Oh, yeah – and, and how about the purple octopus arms reaching up in the field and grabbing the birds and the rabbit?"

"Yep!" affirmed Nina.

"And I suppose the talking dolphin at the beach in Sea City was real?" questioned Piper.

"Absolutely. And remember the Lost Atlantis Plunge ride at the park and when we went forward in time?"

Piper's eyes widened as they walked toward the others. "Yes, and the time we went to the house in the woods on Halloween?"

"Uh-huh, but that wasn't fake. Octella and the monsters were for real – all part of the adventures."

"But I thought that..."

"It was all real. Piper, remember when we ran away from the mansion? Remember the howling sounds of spooks and ghouls, and that crazy wind?"

Nina stopped in her tracks, leaving the others to walk far ahead. "Piper, what did you ask for in your birthday wish last week?"

Piper gave her friend a curious look. Tears welled up in her eyes. "Well, I just wished to know. I wished that, whatever you were hiding from me, I would finally know. After all, you were hiding a lot. That much is certain."

Piper sat on the ground and started to cry as months of suppressed emotion washed over her. Nina knelt beside her and wrapped her arm around her shoulders. After a few minutes, Nina broke the silence.

"I was sworn not to tell you or any other living thing about the lands down here. I was dying to tell you, but I promised not to say a word. And I was also told not to tell you or anyone about Arianna. If I could have, I would have told you – believe me. You are my best friend, and I love you so much."

Piper's sobbing subsided; she looked up at Nina's saddened appearance.

"Hey, you two! Get a move on. We are nearing the barrion pass," yelled Edip from afar.

Yurggie's barks beckoned the girls to catch up with their friends. Kicking up the dusty soil, they continued to reminisce about the wild experiences they had shared.

Within ten minutes they advanced to a vertical crevice in the tall rock wall. The team stopped. Hodges turned to the others.

"We now leave the kingdom. For all of you, each step is a measure into the unknown. I know these paths, and you will have to trust me from this point on. Obey my words and you shall be safe. All talking must be kept to whispers till further notice. Stay close and activate your luminars. The gloaming shall leave us for a time. Stay close and have faith." His words of valor inspired the others.

The starling disappeared into the dark pass with Yurggie by his side. Holding out their luminars, Edip and Enver followed close behind.

Nina Leigh whispered under her breath, "I just hope Arianna is watching nearby."

Chapter Ten

Marauders of the Mind

Tuesday, April 20 (late afternoon)

Navigating through the pass did not seem as long or frightening as the girls had anticipated. The glowing cylinders served to light the way and dispel many fears that troubled their hearts along the harrowing trek. Soon faint illumination appeared farther down the narrow, serrated passageway.

"We have made excellent time, my friends. Behold, the gloaming of the bedloe lands penetrates the pass ahead of us," Hodges declared with a heartening tone in his deep voice.

The Kimonos followed the starling's hand gesture and slowed down about fifty feet from the cleft's opening. The scout signaled to the team to sit in a circle. Yurggie received gentle pats from Enver, who held the cannoid on a leash.

"Friends, this is the gateway to the Bedloe Abidion. Girls, my gnome comrades know of the bedloe. But even their knowledge of these mysterious beings is quite limited. I will tell you this: the bedloe loathe gnomes and their allies, and are a reclusive race. They are mystical shadows with extraordinary powers of mind. No gnomes have actually seen a bedloe and lived to tell of it."

"Heavens, how are we going to get through their land to that swamp Shäbáhn talked about?" Nina asked.

Hodges continued. "We have on our side the advantage of stealth, Yurggie's keen sense of presence, and my experience as a scout. They may eventually sense that we are in their land, but they will not have clarity of whom, where, or when. But the danger lies in the fact that these mindbenders can manipulate thoughts, our thoughts. They can send telepathic messages at random to confuse and confound our efforts. I can only presume they will wish to harm us or trigger our retreat. However, we will not let that happen. We will watch over each other so that reality is not confused with malignant visions from these insidious spinners."

"Spinners?" asked Nina.

Hodges nodded. "Yes, they are spinners. The bedloe exist in our dimension, but not as we do. We are stationary beings moving linearly in space. However, bedloe are not as we are, for they literally spin all the time. Hence, spinners."

With widening eyes Piper asked, "But how will we avoid these bedloe spinning things? Won't we run into them along the way?"

Hodges raised his long eyebrows in disapproval. Enver cleared his throat.

Edip quietly chuckled, saying, "Master Starling, do not be offended. The human girls do not understand your powers and unusual talents."

Edip turned to the girls to explain. "Nina, Piper, please understand that Hodges has the power to impede and cloud telepathy. He is a Master Scout as are those starlings of the Häagen Clan. He is a reconnoiter for valid reasons that you will see along our journey."

"Enough babble concerning me," Hodges said impatiently. "Come, it is time to venture out and beyond. We are many miles east of the fabled cities of Gilgal and Perth. From this region we should be relatively safe from detection." He quickly turned toward the opening with his long coattails flinging about.

Slowly they emerged into a twilight forest. The land's gloaming effect cast an eerie amber radiance from above. Staying close together, they progressed southward along the Eastern Barrion. The hardened clay muffled their footsteps.

Nina and Piper peered all around. Never before had their eyes beheld such lush and alien vegetation. Tall flowering plants like magnificent blue sunflowers poised their faces upward as if satisfaction could be derived from their thirsty reach toward the counterfeit sky. Nina noticed it first; she alerted her friend in a whisper.

"The flowers! Did you see how those huge flowers move like they are looking at us, spying on us?"

"What are you talking about?" Piper whispered back.

Nina grabbed Piper's hand and pointed to the cluster of teal-colored stalks. "See! The flower blossoms are turning as we move by."

"Are you trying to scare the daylights out of me?"

"Shhh!" Edip insisted. "We must not draw attention to ourselves. Your voices can echo off the barrion and travel distances."

"But the flowers have noticed us. They are following us. Just look for yourself." Nina sighed.

Hodges stopped abruptly and swung around to face the frightened girls. "Do not fear the koppyshobba. It follows you because it sees you. The koppyshobba is the closest to intelligent life of any plant on or under the earth. They feel your presence, seek to know you. They will not betray us."

With those words he turned about and quickened his pace. The others moved ahead to catch up. The girls wanted to talk but did not wish to provoke the consternation of the tall, mysterious scout.

Soon the Kimonos passed the abandoned Pillars of Janieros, massive vertical obelisks constructed of gold porcelain, inlaid emeralds, and adamantine steel. The starling stopped to whisper.

"My friends, those are the sacred monuments of the bedloes' past, a time when this race was in harmony with the lands of the north and east. But the pillars have lost their luster and all meaning to these corrupted marauders of the mind."

Piper's gaze was glued to the intricate carvings midway up one of the slender structures. She strained her eyes to see if the chiseled writings were legible. Perhaps the inscriptions would be in English. Without warning, a winged reptilian creature appeared at the pinnacle, its fiery eyes fixed on her alone. In an instant it lunged from its steely perch and swooped downward. Piper's screams went unnoticed as the others walked on with Hodges leading the way.

The dreadful dragon descended and arched for a strafing run. Piper backed up to the jagged barrion. Imprisoned in fear, she covered her eyes with her arms. Vainly she cried for help, but the shrieks merely resonated off the steep canyon walls like spitting flashes from an Independence Day sparkler.

Skimming the jagged wall, the screaming beast clutched the girl. Sharp talons ripped her clothes. Pain shot through her shoulders and back. Piper felt her feet dangling while she was lifted airborne and into the amber twilight. Her ripped backpack sent its contents plummeting to the ground. Maddened by such sudden abduction, she dropped her head down to witness the landscape passing beneath her limp, lifeless legs. She gasped in the thick air. Her chest pounded with horror; she prayed for deliverance. Then all went black.

Her mind was groggy. She could barely open her eyes. Squinting to focus, Piper discerned a rounded, stubby haystack in front of her. Within the mirage willowy silhouettes moved from side to side. At first she thought they were branches from a large shrub disturbed by a wind behind the stack. Slowly her vision cleared. She rose and moved closer to the object while reaching around to cover her exposed, bloody shoulder.

The sudden screeching resounded like banshees from the Emerald Isle. Hideous caws cast clarity into her mind. Three newborn beasts craned their necks in her direction, snapping their heads forward in an attempt to pick at the horrified girl. Piper screamed. Shrieks from behind her caused the lost Kimonian to swing about. Hovering high in the shallow sky, the monstrous mother spiraled downward to her repulsive runts. Trapped and terrified, Piper bobbed her head from side to side, confused and defeated. Once again the monster's talons snatched her by the shoulders, shaking her violently. Before unconsciousness prevailed, the girl's last thoughts were of the hungry beaks that chirped to be fed.

Piper's frame shook severely, but not by shock or ailment. Rather the resolute hands of Hodges tried to revive the tortured girl as she lay stiffened by the trauma. "Piper, Piper, awaken! You are safe with us. We are here. You are among friends," he assured her.

The faint voices nudged Piper into consciousness. Her vision cleared to behold the face of her dearest friend leaning over her.

"Oh, Nina Leigh! I am so glad to see you," Piper cried, clinging to her friend so as not to let go.

"You are safe now. You were a victim of bedloe mind control," said Nina.

"What? But I was here, then gone, then the flying thing, and the nest. I was almost killed!"

Nina smiled, wiping the tears from Piper's reddened face. "The bedloes got to you. But we were here the whole time."

Hodges grabbed her by the knees. "Yes, young friend, we were here all the time. You do not remember. The spinners perceived that we were here and endeavored to destroy each of us through our own buried fears. While we walked onward, you became their first and only victim. It appears that your mind became their playground; you fell prey to their mental invasion."

"But didn't they try to attack you all?" asked Piper.

Hodges grinned. "Starlings are immune to their devices. It was I who pulled you from the traps they laid. You were just too tantalizing to them. Your fears run very deep, Miss Slack."

"Oh, I could have told you that," snickered Nina, looking around to see if the others deemed her comical remark as inappropriate.

Piper cowered. "Will they attack again?"

"No!" asserted the scout. "I have resisted them for now. But we must hurry."

Nina helped Piper to her feet, brushing off her jacket and adjusting her backpack. The starling gestured with his long slender fingers to follow him along the path.

"We are nearly to the end of this territory," he said. "The next pass is hidden behind that cluster of rocks way up ahead. Hug the barrion. We must make haste lest the enemy discover our exact whereabouts and strike again."

Hodges led them behind the strange rocky formation, which hid the slim vertical fracture in the barrion's steep rise.

"Reach for your lights," he said. "We now enter a longer pass that will lead us into the marshlands. A greater challenge lies ahead of us within Creetswarron. It is there we are bound to encounter Old Switch."

"Who's that?" asked Nina with her hand gripping Piper's.

"I will divulge more of it at the end of the passageway. Now follow," beckoned Hodges.

"At least we're leaving those awful bedloes," Piper murmured.

Hodges turned his head and whispered, "The good news is that now you may be permanently immune to the spinners' influence."

The mysterious leader entered the darkness. The others followed in silent wonder.

Chapter Eleven

Creetswarron

Tuesday, April 20 (late evening)

By now the Kimonos was beyond the pass. Humidity hung heavy in the atmosphere. Nina was fascinated by the unusual rockscape and flats. She drew in a deep breath; the air smelled like the marshlands of Cape May County.

The starling raised his slender arm to his comrades with a calming gesture, forewarning them to stay close by his side.

The gloaming effect within this region was much dimmer, painting a dismal gloominess to dismay the most cheerful of sojourners.

Halting their progress, Hodges scanned each anxious soul with his deep, dark eyes.

"This is Creetswarron, the forbidden swamp. Rarely do trespassers breach its borders. Yet, in order to arrive at our destination, we must traverse this soggy and forsaken wasteland, for any other route would take us far out of the way and jeopardize our time to retrieve King Tréfon's daughter."

Nina raised her hand to cradle her chin. Deep in thought, she asked, "What do you mean about the time?"

"The princess must be returned to the kingdom and to the waters no later than the predetermined hour, or else we shall fail in our mission. Edip, Enver, collect the girls' lights and put them in your pockets. We will not need them till later."

"Wait! You still haven't explained to me—"

Nina's inquiry was curtailed by a gentle nudge from Enver and the scout's forward, cautious advance. The ground grew boggier as the Kimonos neared the edge of a verdant knoll. The faint light could not conceal the stagnant marsh that lay ahead in the vast cavernous land. A labyrinth of irregular pathways led in every direction. None but the shrewd scout could fathom how to cross.

Hodges stopped suddenly by a cluster of tall scraggly bushes. "The path through Creetswarron is full of treachery and trickery. I will guide. The way is narrow, demanding that you synchronize your steps with mine. Veering too far to the left or right may result in injury or worse."

The starling reached within one of the bushes and snapped off several dead but sturdy branches measuring about a yard in length.

"Here, carry a rod with you, for you will need it soon enough," he warned.

Edip grabbed the scout's forearm. "Hodges, explain to them about the creature. They must know what lies beneath."

Hodges looked at the girls with compassion. "Yes, I suppose you are correct. Girls, there is a notorious thing that abides below the surface of these putrid pools. Albeit, Old Switch is more than a myth or a legend, for I have witnessed it with my own eyes many years ago. I have felt its foul stroke across my skin. I have borne its anger in my mind," divulged the starling.

"You have seen it? You actually beheld the beast?" Enver said with surprise.

"Aye, I have. Heed these words. You must stay close by my side. Be circumspect; the waters hide malevolence. The creature is sly and will attack the weary and unwatching. If you see it, crack its cruel claws with the rod. That should drive it away from the path for awhile."

"Sir, what will it do to us? I mean, what exactly is it?" asked Piper, who yearned to retreat into the pass that was several hundred feet behind her.

"No one truly understands why Old Switch is ravenous in its pursuit of travelers. Nor does anyone know its origins. We do understand that the reptile delights in the ruination of the naïve and the reckless. Therefore, your due vigilance will improve our chances of safe passage through this squalid slough. Enough words—this conversation delays our advancement."

With that the starling turned and proceeded ahead, giving no opportunity for further discussion. Enver walked behind Hodges and Yurggie; the girls were sandwiched between the two gnomes. Edip was ever vigilant, for he knew he bore the greater responsibility for the safety of his human friends.

The narrow, boggy path that the scout had chosen weaved through the swamp like a twisting sidewinder. If not for Hodges' keen eyes, the exact path would be quite indefinable to the others, whose eyes spied to and fro. Yet the scout's deep, discerning eyes never strayed from the moistened ground in front of him.

Quietly the Kimonos walked onward. With every cautious step, filthy dampness seeped through the seams of their shoes. Only the squishing sounds of their pace could be heard on the spongy trail. Piper nearly hugged Nina's back as she tried to stay close to her best friend. Nina tolerated the annoyance of Piper stepping on her heels every few steps. She understood how frightened Piper had become back in the Abidion. And this strange nightmare was far from over.

A smack and a splash abruptly sliced the silence. The girls ceased their progress as they turned to see that Edip had retracted his rod to his side. To the gnome's left the stagnant waters sluggishly rippled into the teal-colored reeds nearby.

"What was that?" Nina muttered.

She did not want to receive another solemn rebuke from the tall guide. Piper grabbed Nina's hand tightly as both girls awaited a reasonable, less scary answer than they were likely to hear.

With an air of regret, Edip said, "Something grabbed my left ankle. Something very hard and cold tried to get me. By sheer reflex I hit it with my rod. Then it slithered under the surface before I could get a good look."

The astonished girls stood statuesque, wanting not to believe the brief, candid testimony of their stout companion. The starling's brusque voice broke their bewilderment. The girls quickly turned to catch up with the other two while Edip followed behind.

Nina's eyes roamed from side to side as she tried to assess which was more important: losing her footing or losing her courage to the thing that lay in wait just below the oily scum. Her mind succumbed to memories in which gallantry was tested in similar degrees. The lessons indirectly wrought by the measures of the Jêhvahaér were not to be taken lightly. No, the unusual wonders of the previous year would remain indelibly imprinted on Nina's soul even as her boundless imagination surged with perseverance to walk headlong into the heart of peril. And that same contagion infected Piper, although to a lesser measure.

She could not perceive which first deterred her thoughts – the splash or the grip. But Nina knew that Old Switch had made its sudden assault as her foot penetrated the slimy greenness of the stagnant pond. Before the others could react to the cries for help, her left leg sank deeper while the hidden creature yanked. Edip clutched her flailing arms with his broad hands and held on tight. Enver made random strikes at the scum with his rod, trying to avoid hitting the girl's slick leg. Pushing Enver aside, the starling knelt and grasped Nina around the waist with both arms.

Bubbles percolated through the gooeyness as the creature struggled to pull its victim below and away from the others. Hodges intensified his grip. Yurggie growled and woofed. The commotion resonated through the swamp.

Nina screamed in panic. Piper covered her ears to dampen the desperate cries for help.

"Nina! Nina! Cease your resistance. Let me take on the fight," Hodges shouted. "Trust me! You must trust in me now!"

With the scout locked onto her waist, Nina slowly stopped thrashing about. Hodges kept his eyes glued to the thick, turbulent water swirling about her thigh. With the girl firmly anchored in his grip, he released his right arm and extended it over her body and downward toward the buried creature. His palm widened; his outstretched fingers arched as if to invoke a curse.

"Hear me well, Old Switch. Relinquish your hold on this human! I command it by the Order of the Häagen. Release her now or perish!" the starling bellowed with an authority that reverberated throughout the great wet wasteland.

Suddenly the starling's palm shone like the Shekinah glory of old. Mystical beams of light shot down through the grimy surface of the swampwater. At once the struggle ceased. The streams of light ceased. Hodges pulled the terrified girl onto the path while Edip retrieved a towel from his pack.

With a modest grin, Hodges gazed into Nina's troubled eyes. "Now, now, you are safe. I asked you to trust me and you did. I thank you. Old Switch will not harm you now. It has fled."

Nina looked up at her friends, who hovered over her with grave concern etched into their faces. She turned to Hodges and smiled while Edip wiped her slimy leg with the dry cloth.

"I think I'm all right. Would you please help me up, Hodges?" Her voice still held an ebbing tremor.

Grabbing her hands, he raised her off the spongy ground and held her as she steadied herself.

"Now that is something I would not wish on anyone," she quipped. Piper leaned over and embraced Nina.

"Oh, I was so nervous, so worried. I'm glad you're safe," Piper said.

Regaining their composure, the companions turned and walked onward through the swamp. Their newfound mutual confidence was laced with caution. And this form of bravery would serve each of them well in the miles ahead.

Although shrouded by the gloaming effect, the lateness of the hour had dulled the senses and fears of the girls. Yet, between yawns, Nina marveled at what she had witnessed just minutes ago when Hodges delivered her from the gruesome monster.

With her limp subsiding, Nina pondered many things. Who really was this starling? By what means was he able to overcome such a foe? What other powers did he possess? And who was Zandra – most highly revered by her subterranean companions?

Chapter Twelve

The Deadly Rocks

Wednesday, April 21 (early morning)

It was not Piper's snoring that woke Nina but the pain in her back. Not even the meager contents of her knapsack beneath her small frame could render much comfort. With a stiff neck and achy shoulders, she rolled over and stretched her limbs beyond the thin flannel blanket. Arching her feet, she accidentally kicked a sneaker off the uneven ledge and down onto the spongy moss that bordered the horrible marsh. Hodges broke his vigilant gaze over the flats, fixing his dark eyes upon Nina's.

"Do not be afraid. I will retrieve the wayward shoe," whispered the mysterious scout with a lingering grin that Nina had never seen before.

Yurggie remained on the ledge while the starling gracefully climbed down the face of the rocky crag. Nina leaned over the edge to watch his fluid movements, fearing that the unseen slithering thing would pounce on her new friend.

Sensing her anxiety, Hodges peered upwards. "Fret not, Nina. Old Switch is not close by. It will seek other prey besides us. Here now. Catch!"

He hurled the damp white and red canvas shoe up to her waiting hands. Unfortunately, the commotion was enough to stir the others from their imperfect sleep.

"Hey, what's going on?" Piper said with a yawn while the gnomes began to gather their scattered gear.

"By mistake I kicked my shoe and it fell down there. Hodges was kind enough to get it for me."

"But I don't see him," Piper said just as the starling's head emerged from the ledge.

With little conversation, the five finished stuffing their backpacks with the starling exerting the lesser effort.

"Hodges, did you get any sleep last night?" asked Nina.

Edip and Enver turned to her; the starling ignored the inquiry.

"I keep forgetting you do not know him very well. Hodges never sleeps," offered Enver. "It is the nature of all starlings. They are neither affected by fatigue nor ruled by the gloaming."

Edip yawned. "I do not know how he does it, staying awake all night."

Piper wished she had known that small fact many hours ago, for her sleep would have been much more restful.

Soon the Kimonos was ready for the next leg of their mission. With the scout leading the way, they left cavernous Creetswarron behind. After no more than a hundred feet of walking Piper stopped dead in her tracks.

"Yurggie! Hodges, where's Yurggie?" she blurted.

Hodges halted the team and turned. "He is fine. I sent him up ahead to scout the boundary of Tremória. He will meet us at the great chasm before we pass the bluffs and enter the deadly rocks."

"Did you say *deadly* rocks?" asked Piper.

"Shhh, it'll be all right," assured Nina, who held her hand and pulled her along.

The travelers continued their trek with Creetswarron's distant gloaming dimly lighting their path through the narrowing corridor. The rocky walls became more sharp and irregular.

"Stay close to one another. We are nearing the quaking zone," said Hodges in a subdued but serious tone.

Walking in single file made personal dialogue quite inconvenient, yet Nina was compelled to ask a question on behalf of the others.

"Hodges, what exactly is this Tremória place? You mentioned it back at SheeNao Depot but never described it to us."

"It is the region of living rocks. We have no other alternative but to travel through. You see, the Forbidden Bluffs in the west are too steep to traverse. And to the east is the Great Telexian Divide – wide and impregnable. We must proceed straight ahead through this hazard. Quick now. Let us make haste. Soon we will rendezvous with the cannoid."

The team walked onward. Nina's back still ached; Piper's ankles were sore. But the girls quickened their pace, inspired by the tall scout's sense of mission. However, an uncanny feeling that someone was watching their every move permeated each footstep and thought.

The gloaming effect dissipated the farther they traveled from the horrible swamplands. The soggy moss had turned into amber sands. Up ahead the sands metamorphosed into solid, wavy streaks of rough granite. The terracotta colorations were breathtaking.

Commotion from within the underbrush in front of them sent shivers down the girls' spines. They flew into each other's arms as something emerged from the sparse teal vegetation.

"Yurggie! Good," called Hodges as the tracking animal leaped up to greet his master. "Tell Hodges what he needs to know, my little friend."

The scout knelt and inclined his ear toward Yurggie's licking tongue. Petting from his master's hand settled the creature. Muffled yaps conveyed a secret language that only the starling understood. The girls were mesmerized by the scene as Hodges and his furry companion conversed so freely. Piper's left eyebrow arched up in curiosity.

"Wow! What do you make of that?" she asked.

Enver's interruption was polite. "Hodges is full of wonder and mystery, if I may say so myself. In fact, we gnomes regard those of the Häagen Clan as demigods to some degree."

Hodges looked over at Enver and shook his head in slight disapproval. "In myself I am nothing. I am but a servant to the Ancient of Days, the Father of Lights."

The starling stood and turned to the others to disclose the information. "Yurggie tells me the intervals are in twenties. I was hoping for more, but this will do for our purposes. Yes, timing will work to our advantage."

"Would you mind telling us what in the world you're talking about?" Nina said with growing impatience.

Hodges looked into her wide hazel eyes.

"Ah yes. Follow me to the mouth of the tunnel up ahead. For your own safety, I will instruct you there on what you need to do. You see, timing is everything."

The Kimonos followed their leader in quiet anticipation. At the entrance the rocky wall split into a vertical zigzag formation. The scout stopped and bid them to rest on the dark bedrock.

"We are about to enter Tremória. The passage we will tread is less than one mile. Yet it is a treacherous stretch. If we are successful, we should pass through the barrion in a couple of hours — hopefully less. However, the risks we face are extreme and potentially deadly."

The team sat and stared at the scout without blinking. Even the cannoid stood in silence as if muted by the stark facts. Hodges sat down, completing the asymmetrical circle. His eyes widened; his mouth stiffened.

"I tell you this. The walls within the tunnel are alive and lethal. Because of the magnetic fields and seismic fluxes created by the great waters above and the volcanic rivers below, dimensional distortions run amok in Tremória. What I mean to say is that the very rocks tend to phase and falter on predictable, rhythmic cycles. The phasing causes dimensional shifts while the faltering produces spatial transference.

"You *must* follow my footprints within the passageway. Therefore, fix your vision on the footsteps of the person in front of you. My steps will create the right path, the right pattern. If we walk in synchrony, then the visual distortions around us will have no ill effect on our progress.

"Now remember, if you look up, behind, or side to side, you will risk being deceived and beguiled. If you stray off course, you will place yourself in harm's way."

Piper nervously asked, "But what if we look up by accident during the distortion – when the thing's occurring?"

Hodges' facial expression announced it clearly. "My dear Piper, you will not stray from the right path if you heed my words. But if you should follow another path, the end thereof may be death. You see, when the phasing and faltering is completed, you might find yourself entombed in solid rock."

A hush fell upon the team. Hodges stood and smiled. "The good news is that the sand coating the tunnel's floor is at least an inch thick. Therefore, we will have success moving through the passage—that is, if each one exercises the gravest temperance."

With that he signaled them to enter into the dark tunnel. With luminars in hand they marched bravely toward the living rocks.

Nina followed Piper to keep an eye on each of her steps as well as her own. Though tempted, the girls never talked, for it seemed inappropriate under the extreme circumstances, which mandated the strictest circumspection.

The handheld lights cast eerie shadows on the scarred interior, making the enclosure even spookier. Fear welled up in Piper's heart. How she longed to stop and turn to her friend. But the stern admonition from Hodges echoed within her soul. Only the shushing sounds of shoes on sand would be her solace along the way.

Each pair of eyes attended the footprints ahead as the members tried to place their feet exactly within the imprints in the sand. Despite everyone's diligence, the feeling that something dreadful was about to happen nagged and gnawed at their emotions. Only the Vulcan-like leader seemed immune to these tugging doubts of despair.

A scraping sound behind Nina shattered the silence. She spun around to see the end of the line. Enver had vanished! She gave a startled cry, and the others halted their walking and turned.

"I told you to keep your eyes to the ground! You know the rules. Why have you defied my warnings?" yelled the starling.

Nina turned her head just enough to eye the scout. "Do you think I'm playing around? For heaven's sake, Enver is gone! He just disappeared!"

Immediately the scout made his way to the end of the line, peering about into the rocky walls that could imprison them all.

"He's not gone. Look to the left," Hodges said with an uncharacteristic quiver in his voice.

The wall he pointed to was slightly transparent, revealing the silhouette of a lost and frightened Enver, who was desperately trying to find sanctuary from a crushing peril.

Weeping in anguish, Edip ran to the wall and pounded on it as if the rocky rampart would obey his demands to yield. Hodges pulled the gnome back with the rest. Yurggie's sudden howls echoed through the tunnel like a siren of impending doom.

"Our strength cannot help our friend; faith will be our ally at this moment of need," the scout said with a growing apprehension in his voice.

Piper stood speechless, horrified. Nina pondered the wise words, for she knew that she could lean on Him who could be fully trusted during times of trials. It was the Old Testament memory verse from the prophet Nahum to which she clung – that the Lord is good, a stronghold during fiery ordeals; and He knows those that trust in Him.

Withdrawing a small silver box from his coat pocket, Hodges held it loosely in his palm. All eyes fell on its unusual, ornate beauty. Rubies surrounded the ends. Diamonds functioned as activators. The starling pointed the object toward Enver, who helplessly and soundlessly begged for rescue behind the solidifying rock. The scout pressed several jewels in figure-eight patterns. A small panel slid open on the object's side, revealing coordinates and readings.

"This indicates that the next transition will be in exactly one minute. The three of you and Yurggie must stand over by the crook in the wall across the way to avoid being trapped. I will remain here to retrieve Enver if I can."

How he gained this information, no one knew. Edip and the girls sensed his wisdom and followed suit. Against the other wall they huddled in fearful anticipation. Meanwhile, the starling refocused his attention back on the barrier that separated the trapped gnome from his worried comrades.

"Can you save him? Can you get him out?" cried Piper.

The tall scout spoke not a word. Meanwhile, Edip's gentle strokes on her long wavy hair provided Piper some solace.

"He knows what he is doing. Like I told you before, the Häagen are full of mystery and miracles," Edip offered with a sigh of hope.

Nina gazed at the other two across the tunnel. Her admiration for the revered rescuer swelled. This was not the first time that Hodges had risked his life for a friend. The courage and strength of his convictions knew no bounds.

Facing Enver, Hodges warned the others. "Within seconds the distortions will occur; do not move. Do not be deceived by what you see. Just stay put!"

The three remained in a tight hugging position. Suddenly and silently the rock which had encased Enver phased again. Hodges grabbed the frightened gnome and cradled him in his arms. While the Kimonos remained statuesque, the walls of rock that lined the cave danced and darted about. The visual effect was so stunning the girls immediately became queasy as if they were on a twirling amusement park ride. They had not been bothered by the horrid effect before because looking at the ground disallowed the sickening effects of the distortions.

Soon the walls returned to their normal state. Holding Enver, Hodges tried to lower him to the ground, but the gnome hugged the scout's torso and cried in gratitude. Hodges embraced his friend and whispered in another language.

Turning to the others, the starling spoke. "Come, let us return to our course. Remember, my friends, remain focused on the right path!"

The five weary members and the cannoid continued on through the treacherous passage of Tremória. A short way ahead would provide a brief and needed respite. And time was running out for the imprisoned and fading heir to the throne.

Chapter Thirteen

Ílda-dunn Crossing

Wednesday, April 21 (midday)

Just beyond the mouth of the tunnel from where they exited, Hodges beseeched them to sit in a tight circle on a blue grassy mound. The rushing sounds of an unseen river filled the air. Stopping for a break pleased the entire crew, especially the girls, who were famished and exhausted from the miles of rough terrain. The rest brought sighs of relief, for their arches and shins ached from the relentless pace maintained by the scout.

The gloaming effect had returned on this other side. One by one they pocketed their bronze luminars. Edip slid off his backpack and placed it in front of him. His broad, callous hands fiddled with the strap that held down the flap. Once the pack was opened, he reached for the edibles that were neatly wrapped in cellophane. With a grin he offered portions to the girls first, then the others. Yurggie yipped for a morsel of the sweet treat.

"Don't we have anything else to nibble on besides these periwinkle waffles and thick syrup? I'm getting tired of eating the same thing for every meal," said Piper, pouting and protesting with her arms folded.

"It is periwafers with Seldarian honey, which is quite sweet and delicious. Come on, Piper. Take some for the sake of nourishment," said Edip, enticing her with his hands posed in a prayerful gesture. Rolling her eyes, she grabbed the wrapped wafer and the rigid container.

"As you can hear, around the corner up ahead is a river called Rippicon. While we rest, take the time to replenish your canteens before we leave this area," said Hodges.

"Where's all the water coming from?" asked Nina.

Hodges closed his eyes and sighed. "The body of water which you refer to as the Delaware Bay supplies the Rippicon River. However, the Rippicon is not brackish but sweet and pure. You will find it most pleasing."

As they ate their meager meal, small talk precluded anything with meaningful substance. Despite their sore lower limbs, the girls were full of energy.

"Hodges, I don't get it. We've walked mile after mile with very little sleep from last night – if you can call it night. Yet I don't feel sleepy as I would expect to feel. Why is that?" Nina asked.

The starling wiped his mouth and paused, placing his trash in a clear bag by Edip's backpack. "It is a reasonable question to ask. You see, because you are closer to the Earth's center, gravity is slightly weaker. Further, oxygen seeks lower levels, thus making the air richer in many parts of the underlands, including this region. These are contributing factors for not feeling fatigued."

"Not to change the subject, but on a more important note, what about the trolls?" Piper said. "Are you still convinced they are the main ones behind the plot to kidnap the princess? Why do you think it's them and not just Borok and his gang?"

The starling leaned forward and looked intently into her eyes. "Remember, the kandalarians are being used. It is

Shaptillicus who detests the gnomes the most and is likely the one who has orchestrated the abduction."

"But why?" Nina asked.

"Ah! That, my dear one, is a jewel of a question. And thank you for redirecting our thoughts to the main mission of this group. With the kidnapping and possible subsequent death of Tréfon's daughter, the trolls are convinced that the gnomes' kingdom will tumble in confusion and despair. I believe the trolls are hoping the gnomes will swiftly retaliate against them. This will give Shaptillicus a clear advantage to strike out against the little people. In other words, war and invasion!

"Further, my intuition tells me that Shaptillicus is assuming the gnomen allies will not risk the peace in order to defend the little people. And without help from their allies, the gnomes would be doomed to defeat in a battle against the trolls, the gozzi, and the goblins.

"You see, Shaptillicus is ruthless and deliberate in his desires to conquer the First Kingdom, which has been a thorn in the side of his wicked dynasty. Therefore, it is imperative that we fail not in the rescue."

"But you still haven't answered why the trolls hate the gnomes so much," insisted Nina.

"As I have said before, it is hate for hate's sake!" affirmed the scout. "Hate knows no bounds; it is cold and calculating and jealously feeds upon hate. You see, the gnomes stand in the way. It is the rich, fertile land, the Zander Zee, and the promise that the trolls desire. And whoever possesses the promise can easily control the kingdom and all of Gilacia and beyond!"

The girls were eager to inquire into the convoluted political affairs of these subterranean lands. But what haunted Piper the most was Cirlaena, for she knew that Her Highness' life was linked to her safe and timely return to the kingdom. But why? What powerful force bound the princess to the gnomen homeland to the point of her own peril? What secret held the little people to the boundaries of their beloved lands?

Feeling that her quota for questioning had expired, Piper looked at Nina, hoping that she would continue the vein of conversation. However, Nina just stared beyond Hodges and Piper, as if contemplating deeper thoughts.

Hodges stood, smiled, and chuckled to himself. Oddly, he softly sang what seemed to resemble a Celtic hymn:

> *We're following a magic tune*
> *The piper's song we sing,*
> *To venture into distant lands*
> *And liberation bring.*

Gathering his things, the tall one turned and walked on toward the surging sounds. The others quickly gathered their belongings and followed the wise scout. Rounding the stony edifice, the team collectively beheld the swift flowing waters of Rippicon. The crystal clear river rustled with small gurgling waves that licked at the eroded banks, hungering to venture beyond. While the team filled their canteens by the river's edge, Piper tapped on Hodges' shoulder.

"That song – it's so pretty. Did you make it up?"

The starling smiled. "No. The melody is of the mêdebáhn."

"What does it mean?"

"It means that the world is full of hope, full of poetry. Within the rhyme lies significance to those who will truly listen."

Piper pondered his words while gazing at the rushing river. She turned to him with wide eyes. "Is the message for us?"

He stood and glanced about as if ignoring her. "The message *and* melody are for the piper."

99

The starling walked ahead with the others following. Piper was not able to discern if he had succumbed to rudeness or mere candor.

A narrow trail hugged the ridge to their right; the Rippicon splashed over the bank to the left. The arched cavern ceiling overhead followed the river as if it had been intentionally excavated by subterranean miners.

"You will need your luminars along the riverbank. We will not encounter the gloaming until we have passed through the crossing up ahead," forewarned the scout as he reached into his deep coat pocket to retrieve the shiny device.

One by one they actuated the lights, which filled the huge, elongated enclosure with brilliance. Colorful jewels danced and dazzled in the ceiling crevices. The girls cocked their heads back to enjoy the spectral glitter until Piper accidentally stumbled into Enver.

From behind, Edip said, "Girls, you both best keep your eyes on the path, because our duties do not include rescuing clumsy travelers who fall into the river."

"But it's so beautiful," said Piper.

"Please keep up," called the starling.

The tunnel weaved slightly to the left and then to the right. Several hundred feet in front of them they could see the stone bridge of Ílda-dunn arching across the surging currents below.

"We will soon be at Ílda-dunn Crossing," bellowed Hodges.

The sound of the river and the echoing effects of the cavern stifled any desire to engage in idle chatter until Piper could not contain herself anymore.

"Hodges! Oh, Hodges! Who built that bridge?" she yelled to the front of the single-file line.

Turning his head toward the river, he replied loudly, "The races who used to inhabit this portion of the Direlands constructed the bridge as a symbol of their quest for peace between their peoples. The Íldanians lived beyond the northern banklands where we are; the Dunndees dwelled south of the river. But that was centuries ago. Both races have long since moved on to safer, more peaceful lands. This old bridge remains as a monument to their coexistence. It is a shame that the bridge has fallen into such disrepair. This is why few travelers come this way."

One by one they turned left and made their short trek to the pinnacle of the cobblestone crossing, which rose nearly twenty feet above the River Rippicon. Sections of the hip-high walls that lined the bridge had fallen into the rushing waters years ago, making the path treacherous and frightening. However, the starling's fixed determination manifested itself in his steadfast, persistent progress.

As they approached the other side, horrid chirping and screeching sounds bellowed from upriver. Hodges quickly huddled the team on the wet rocks of the southern bank.

"We have been fortunate, albeit the vampire bats are awakening from their hibernation. They will soon fly westerly and attack. We must make haste."

Returning to single-file formation, the team followed Hodges into a narrow gorge that twisted and turned. But the scout was not confused for he knew the science of magnetic fields, which guided his steps.

Suddenly, an indescribable, oppressive loneliness enveloped the girls that they had not experienced on this journey thus far. This despairing wave washed over their thoughts and emotions. It was only their newfound faith in their leader that strengthened them not to give up hope and the courage of their commitment. With eyes on the tall, mysterious starling, they marched on.

Chapter Fourteen

A Hopeful Horizon

Wednesday, April 21 (late afternoon)

Wretched, sickening thoughts of the boreworms consumed their imaginations. In some respects, Piper
and Nina wished that Hodges had not told them how the
slimy larvae fall from the rocky ceilings and bore into their
victim. The numbing bite, followed by sudden, agonizing
swelling and memory loss, was scary enough. However,

the thought of the worm slithering into its host to gorge and mutilate was frightening beyond words.

The worms were the immediate danger now that the Kimonos had exited the corridor that connected Ílda-dunn Crossing with the desolate, petrified glades of Semmi-Obeedo. Yet the foreign landscape that lay before them for a few miles ahead was the last leg of the journey that separated them from the realm of Kandalar and the imprisoned gnomen princess.

With the scout leading the way the team weaved along the matted path, lined on both sides by the tall, spiked fronds of the dukie plant. Dense, dead foliage denied each sojourner any vista other than the ugly barb-tipped, petrified branches. Nina did not know if it was the narrow trail or the threat of the hidden worms above that made her feel claustrophobic. Her eyes found slight solace in the dark teal horizon ahead that breathed hope of the glades' southern boundary.

"At least we won't have to be too long in this stupid place," blurted Nina as she joined the others, who were bobbing their heads from side to side watching for the worms.

"Yeah!" Piper exclaimed. "I'm getting a headache trying to watch the trail and keep on the lookout for those gross things above us. Hodges, I haven't seen any worms up there. Do you think they're still there?"

"Oh, there is no doubt the boreworms are above us. They are so well hidden that you can only see them protrude like obese fingers from the rock just seconds before they drop. Yes, they sense we are here. But do not look directly above you. Look several feet above and in front of you. They time their attacks with unusual precision."

"Did you have to say that? Now I'm really scared to death," moaned Piper.

"Luckily we'll be out of here soon. Look ahead. I can see the barrion boundary," offered Nina with confidence.

Hodges cleared his throat. "Do not be too quick to surmise that which might seem obvious to the untrained traveler. The horizon appears to be near when in fact it is nearly twice as far in distance."

"Oh great – that's just great," Piper complained.

"Well, at least we have some gloaming to help us see more clearly," said Nina, stroking her wavy brunette hair to check for crawly things.

On and on the Kimonos walked. The monotony of the bland and steady trail was overshadowed by the vigilance to which the endangered members quietly committed. Each peril on their quest wrapped them like invisible, steely fetters, binding both their souls and spirits to one another. Doubt, distress, and dread would find these bonds a formidable bulwark to overcome.

Edip kept a constant eye on the tall ceiling. His taking up the rear was quite deliberate, for as guardian Edip bore the greatest burden for the safety of the girls. If any injury befell them, he would carry scars of unforgiveness – not because of a transgression but for fear of his own failure. And no propitiation would suffice if evil befell his human friends.

"Behold the ceiling ahead. They are aroused!" whispered the starling. "They are ready to drop. Dodge them and move on. They cannot crawl to follow. And do not step on them. Just leave them to the glades."

From uneven rocks above the boreworms slithered down like pallid appendages being pushed through the jagged cracks. One by one they dropped on the trail. The team's pace hastened as each person buoyed about to avoid the slugs. Yurggie growled and twisted when one landed on the fur of his neck. The scout swatted the thing into the fronds and kept the forward momentum. Suddenly Nina was smacked on the shoulder from behind.

"Ouch! Cut it out," she snipped as she turned to Edip, who wore a worried face. Immediately she apologized and faced forward, for she knew that the gnome had whisked a slithering worm from her shoulder and toward the dukie.

Hunger and thirst now stalked the Kimonos. But those needs could not be satisfied in the glades. They were sorely engaged in walking and whacking. The large wiggling maggots fell like sporadic snowfall. Piper's singular thought was that it was only a matter of time till one of them met the misfortune of the bitter bite. Enver yielded to the task of watching out for Hodges, then Yurggie, and then himself, for Enver knew that the scout was absorbed on the horizon, and the cannoid was defenseless and more susceptible to the danger.

"My friends, we are close to the end. Look up ahead," Hodges said with a tremor in his voice. "Soon we can leave these forsaken glades, and then we can find rest from our travels before the eventide."

The words ushered hope and peace for the others while they moved onward toward the bleak barrion. The crisp crackle and snapping of fronds followed by a dull thud caught Nina's attention. She whipped about to see Edip's legs jutting out toward the path. Her screams stopped the team in its tracks. Enver ran to his friend and yanked him onto the trail. Edip had been bitten on the neck. Enver reached for the foul thing that was desperately trying to burrow into its victim. With a firm grasp, Enver snatched the worm from the wound and threw it down into the dense overgrowth. Edip writhed in pain. Enver shook him by the shoulders.

"Edip! Edip! Are you all right, my friend? Answer me now," begged Enver.

Observing Edip's blank, frightened expression, the huddled group realized that the prostrated gnome had lost his thoughts. As much as their concerns could be focused on the ailing gnome, they continued to gaze about and evade the pasty slinkers.

"Enver, you must pick him up and carry him to safety," commanded Hodges. "Do not tarry."

Enver bent down and rolled Edip over his shoulder.

"Let us make haste lest we have another victim," warned Hodges.

The rescuers renewed their forward advance. Carried by a weary Enver, Edip was noticeably quiet. But the wounded friend created no true burden, for dear friends would not view it in that manner. Piper and Nina followed behind, mindfully watching over each other and the gnomes. Imminent danger hung over the Kimonos, for each knew the disadvantage and vulnerability of their terrifying trek. Each pair of eyes yearned for the rise of the rocky boundary of Semmi-Obeedo. But even this end could not vanquish the hidden fears of the wretched bite.

Piper felt the awful sensation of squirming, stubby legs just before the terrible sting – sharp and deep. Delirium clouded her emotions while hungry teeth sliced and gnawed into her tender flesh. Just before she collapsed onto the matted path, Piper's memory faded into nebulous nonsense. The victim lay helpless while the abominable gastropod prepared to feast.

Sensing her friend's absence, Nina instinctively spun around and witnessed her closest friend squirming on the ground, as if overpowered by a strange epileptic fit. Nina pounced upon Piper, rolling her from side to side in order to find the ugly worm that was hidden under Piper's long wavy hair at the nape of her neck. The dripping blood behind Piper's right ear drew Nina's hand to the loathsome parasite, which she snatched and flung with utter contempt. Piper gazed into Nina's eyes. A faint smile faded; her mind slipped into unconsciousness.

All around the worms intensified their uncoordinated assault. The starling's harsh orders spurred Nina into action. Mimicking Enver, she leaned forward, pulling Piper up by the arms. Squatting, Nina struggled to angle Piper over her shoulder. With strained effort she hoisted Piper's quivering body. She was about to hurl a reprimand at Hodges when she saw that the cannoid was cradled in the lanky arms of the scout.

"Sorry that I am unable to help, but Yurggie was bitten as well," uttered the starling.

Hodges, Enver, and Nina slumped onward with the boundary looming dead ahead less than one hundred feet. Their silent anthem resounded with unspoken truth: friends bearing the burden of friends. And the willing acceptance of such burdens would foster love and respect to weather the most dreadful storms.

Soon they were in the safety of the cool inner passageway that led through the huge barrion. Turning to the other two walkers, the scout removed the luminar from his coat pocket with his free hand. The glow filled the dark corridor with a welcome warmth and hope.

"We will need to move deeper into the passage where we will rest and nourish ourselves," he said.

Nina's arms were aching beyond measure. "Can we hurry? I don't think I can carry her much farther."

The scout drew to her side and touched her shoulder. His hand glowed with energy. Immediately her frame was strengthened by the strange power of the starling. Withdrawing his hand, he turned and walked onward, with the others transfixed in his wondrous wake.

Chapter Fifteen

Darkondusk

Wednesday, April 21 (eventide)

R uled by Dark Lord Borok, Darkondusk bore the repu-
tation of malevolence and malignancy in the regions
surrounding the Direlands. The starling knew of Borok, who
was regarded as both beast and legend. His reign was cruel
and totalitarian. Allies and enemies alike quaked at the men-

tion of his name. The shrewd and sensible avoided his presence and wrath at all costs.

Positioned in the northern region of Kandalar, Castle Darkondusk held strategic importance to all who wished ill will against the gnomes and their allies. The magnificent rock-hewn fortress guarded the main access corridors to the southern parts of the underlands, while providing the dark lord and his dubious allies the perfect platform from which to launch offensive strikes.

For centuries Darkondusk had been the instrument to plunder and kill the innocent, and the chief cause of the gnomen Great Migration of 1689. The aged, burly despot had driven many gnomes back to the Prime Kingdom far to the east. Even the inhabitants of the Rippicon found no peace until their great exodus in 1754. Yes, nothing stirred more emotions in the gnomen heart than the thought of the devil of Darkondusk, who delivered desolation to all his enemies.

Yet, by a strange twist of destiny, Trollian Emperor Shaptillicus had called upon the evil, unpredictable tyrant, soliciting his sinister services against the kind diminutives in the north. Such motivation had been driven by unquenchable hate and insatiable guile. And this evil alliance would be sustained, but only for a season.

Although the gloaming effect was similar in intensity within the lands of the Abidion, Creetswarron, and Semmi-Obeedo, an indefinable dreariness shrouded the refreshed members as they emerged from the dark tunnel. The Dominion of Kandalar was marked by peculiar, tangible gloom that cut into shadows like a knife that would defy even Hippocrates' sacred intention. Wicked oppression met each rescuer. In her mind Piper likened the feeling to pressure upon tender ears in deep water. Her fingers gently probed the tender skin behind her right ear where the awful wound was miraculously healed by her tall friend.

Nina and Piper dared not breathe a word as to violate the strict instructions from the starling. Notwithstanding, it was no secret that time was running out for Princess Cirlaena. The journey had been long and treacherous. The two days stretched out like an eternity.

The girls pondered how the rescue team could possibly find the dungeon, secure the prisoner, and retreat to the First Kingdom in time to save her. Faith in the starling was all they had to cling to. In their hearts they believed in his wisdom and words, despite the doubts that assailed such amateur logic.

Stopping near a cluster of stalagmites, the scout turned and signaled for the team to sit in a circle. While they reclined, he knelt with solemn, cold stares. Yurggie faced southward with a low, guttural growl.

"The path ahead is less treacherous but more conspicuous for us to be spotted by the enemy," explained Hodges. "We will proceed together toward the east side of the fortress where the moat breaks into a stream. From there we will wade in the bitter waters that lead into the lowest levels of the stronghold."

"But won't we be seen that close to the castle?" asked Nina.

"I do not believe so, for I shall create a dindólio which will completely deceive the enemy."

Edip chuckled to himself at the girl's bewilderment. "A dindólio is a diversion with supernatural powers. What Hodges means to say is that he will do something quite unusual to fool Borok and his devils."

Hodges stood and bid the Kimonos to follow quietly. The group soon rounded the rocky spikes and followed the rough path into the valley, a wasteland of gray and gloom. Far ahead loomed the horrible castle, which rose high upon the bluffs. The twisted spires nearly touched the shallow sky. Black flags with reddish markings hung lifelessly from poles atop the pinnacles.

The girls and gnomes did not notice the dreadful things till the Kimomos neared the break just before the snaky moat. Perched high on the towers were dark, watchful creatures that resembled giant ravens. Hodges stopped in his tracks; the others huddled by his side. Withdrawing his arm from the green trenchcoat, he lifted his hand as if to silence a crowd. Suddenly the beasts swarmed to the west, converging in a dark, vanishing mass.

The scout turned to the girls by his side, winked mischievously, and proceeded into the stagnant waters that stirred their first in months. Piper was glad the moat rose only to her lower thighs, yet she watched Hodges' movements to see if the moat grew deeper.

The narrow opening at the rocky base drew the scout like a magnet. Standing inside the darkness, the starling instructed the others not to activate their luminars, for he alone would hold the light. The dark, murky corridor cut through the rock haphazardly. That the scout knew his bearings temporarily calmed the girls' fears. How could he know the way? How could he see beyond the curves and bends?

The moat waters led to a huge, cylindrical chamber. Hugging its sides was a winding stairwell cut within the mossy block walls.

Motioning to the others to gather, Hodges gazed into each pair of eager eyes. "We are at the foundation. We must now ascend into the center of this place. No one is to make a sound."

Turning to the moldy steps, Hodges cautiously led the team upward. The girls clung to each other as much as two could in such a perilous position. Slowly they climbed with nothing but the starling's light to guide their destiny.

At the stairwell's end stood a small ledge with a large metal door that led into the bowels of the fortress. With his hand extended over the large, rusted padlock, the mysterious scout uttered something in another tongue. The lock obeyed the foreign words and dropped into his other hand. The door begrudgingly swung open, revealing a huge room with multiple stairs leading upward into Darkondusk.

Without hesitation, Hodges moved to the left with incredible stealth and speed. In soggy clothing and shoes, the others followed. They tried not to stumble upon the archaic rubble scattered about. Up an unknown flight of stone stairs the Kimonos climbed till another level was reached. The starling turned to the right and slid down a dank corridor lined with long, hanging mirrors. The others moved ahead, trying to remain in the vanishing light.

Turning a corner, the team found multiple iron doors that lined the narrow hall. Finally, they had arrived at the notorious dungeon.

"Silence!" commanded the scout in a whisper. Staring about, he stopped at one panel and stooped to peer through the bars, which revealed a small, horrible room. "Princess, are you there?" A faint feminine echo wafted down the dark corridor.

The others gathered next to the bent figure, who seemed perplexed to hear another sound. Hodges stood and lurched ahead, checking each cell for some hint of life. Nearly halfway down the passageway he stood as a statue. Again the sensitive ears of the Häagen had heard the slight whimpers of pain and despair.

Running to the corridor's end, he swung about and stooped to confirm what he suspected. With the other witnesses surrounding him, Hodges held the luminar high with his left hand and touched the lock mechanism with his right. A grinding sound released the lock; the door creaked open to reveal the fading princess lying prostrate on the filthy ground.

"She's dead! She's dead!" whispered Piper in a burst of unrestrained grief.

"Hush now!" chided Enver.

Nearly moving in slow motion, Hodges approached the dying prisoner. Edip withdrew his luminar from his coat pocket. The darkness lapped at the illumination, hungering to extinguish the beautiful rays. While the others peered in from the narrow entrance, the scout knelt by the princess. With his hands cupped around her neck, she stirred.

"Oh no, dear Piper. She is quite alive," announced Hodges with a grim smile. "But we must act quickly and return Princess Cirlaena to the waters."

"The waters? What *is* it with waters? How will that help Cirlaena?" asked Nina.

"The Zander Zee holds the cure. The river is her remedy," Hodges said, staring back down at a diminished loveliness ravished by the crime.

Enver unexpectedly shoved Edip and the girls from the doorway and into the cell. But the awkward maneuver was not of his doing. The slamming of the rusted metal panel heralded a greater gloom, for the disturbance was followed by the most hideous evil cackle the prisoners had ever heard.

"Aha! Aha! At last I possess what I have truly wanted!" came the cruel words of an obscure figure. The starling rose and approached the bars with his light. Leaning forward a bit, he saw the grotesque features of the dark lord himself.

"Borok. Finally we meet," Hodges said with surprising confidence.

"Yes, starling. I assume you are the renowned High One of the Häagen. At least that is what my sources state."

"I am he."

The tyrant mocked. "What a shame. You see, I have known all along. You might say that I have known too much. Your attempts to cloud me have been unsuccessful, as you can see, for I have seen through it all too darkly. And now you are my prisoner, including those two small, worthless things."

Hiding behind the gnomes could neither preclude the girls from being seen nor absolve them from an unjust indictment.

"Ah! And how unusual, how amusing to have two human females as my captives. How wickedly delightful! Step forward!" the fiend demanded.

Nina and Piper emerged from behind the gnomes, who had tried to conceal them the best they could. Quaking in fright, the best friends stood side by side, holding each other's hand – a small but needed comfort.

Nina stuttered, "Please, sir, let us out of here. We mean you no harm. I wish you would just..."

"Silence!" issued the dark lord. "You are here, and here you will live out your days, as few as those days may be."

With that he turned toward his fat adjutant, who had suddenly materialized with other hideous kandalarians warriors.

"Bumpus, you know what to do," said Borok.

"You must know that you cannot contain me," announced the impatient scout.

"Ha! I am amused by your misguided confidence. I must have mistaken your noted wisdom for utter folly," ridiculed the dark lord.

"Borok, you will *not* succeed in your evil endeavors. I am giving you an opportunity to free us and live."

"My, my – the prisoner is dictating terms," laughed Borok as he turned to his subordinates.

"Last chance, kandalarian!" warned Hodges.

"Enough of these pointless words. And do not attempt to manipulate the lock, for I have sealed this door with the Staff of Sandoval. None of you can reach it through the bars save you, starling. Oh – and I might add this disheartening fact – although you can reach the staff, I have wished that it will not concede your efforts. So in essence, you are powerless, Häagen.

"Now if you will kindly excuse me, I have an invasion to plan and lands to conquer. Enjoy your miserable stay. Who now will rescue the rescuers?"

Sickening laughter saturated the dungeon as the smelly kandalarians walked away to join their minions in the upper parts of the stronghold.

Hodges stood by the door. The other four slumped onto the cold slab. Edip's luminar rolled out of his hand and on the grimy ground. The starling joined them, reclining by the princess. His gentle fingers caressed Cirlaena's hair. She sighed in serenity, knowing that her peril may not be as imminent.

"Hodges, what's up with this staff? What is that creepy Borok talking about?" asked Nina.

"He refers to the staff of power. You see, ages ago the ancient Lúboffs and Ŷvódees lived in the northeast region of the gnomen lands. Before the ancients migrated deeper into the Earth, the Lúboff leader, Arch Sandoval, performed a marvelous task – a grand, selfless deed for Zia Zandra."

"And who is this Zandra that everyone talks about?" asked Piper.

"All in due time, Piper. In return of this altruistic gesture, Zia Zandra gave Arch Sandoval a magnificent treasure—a blessing with the staff of power. And whosoever has the staff possesses its mighty power."

"What does the power do?" inquired Nina.

"Is it like a magic wand?" asked Piper

The guide shook his head. "According to the ancient writings, whosoever holds the Staff of Sandoval wields the power to wish for anything – good or evil. Legend has it that, just before the two races left the valley, Sandoval laid the staff into the zee or river and blessed it in honor of the gift-giver. Ever since, the inhabitants of all of Gilacia believe that the staff has remained somewhere in the waters of the Zander Zee.

"So the river is special?" inserted Nina.

"Yes. However, in recent years rumors abounded that the mysterious staff was actually found. It is quite troubling that Borok now is its possessor."

"But what now?" asked Piper.

Nina raised her brow. "Hodges, you have great powers. We've all seen what you can do. Can't you overpower the staff and get us out of here?"

The starling again lowered his head and comforted the ailing princess with gentle strokes. "It is a fact that my people have great authority. But I cannot overcome the power of the Staff of Sandoval. No one on Earth can."

Piper suddenly spun around. "Yurggie! Hodges, where's Yurggie?"

Enver looked up from the cracked, cobbled floor. "He was right by my side before I was pushed in. I know it. I remember clearly."

"But he's missing!" wailed Piper, peering through the iron bars.

All eyes were on the stately scout as if he knew the answer to an awaking secret. He cracked a sly smile.

"I must admit I am surprised that you all have such little faith – perhaps the size of a guato seed. Have you not heard that faith is the substance of things one hopes for, the evidence of the invisible?"

With hands on her hips and impatience in her voice, Nina confronted the leader. "Where *is* Yurggie, and what is to become of us? Tomorrow we could all be dead!"

The somber scout stood and breathed deeply. Bowing his head, he uttered, "Do not permit your faith to be overcome by fear. Do not worry about what might happen tomorrow, for sufficient is this day and its own evil."

Hearing the mild rebuke, the team remained speechless while the wise one returned his razor gaze to the princess. He knelt and cupped his hand under her neck; white light radiated from her long silky hair. The others looked on, not fully understanding the meaning of the scout's brief and strange homily.

Chapter Sixteen

Night Visions

Later that same evening

Nothing could redeem the sleepless hours which worry inhabited and nightmares ruled. Emotions were on edge; nerves were frayed. The girls huddled together in the corner of the dark cell, each trying to keep warm, each trying to fall into restless episodes of sleep.

Nina whispered, "Piper, would you mind reaching over and handing me my backpack? I'm cold and want my blanket."

"Why don't you get it yourself," came the terse reply.

"Since when have you turned into a creep?" huffed Nina.

"Me – a creep? Look who's talking," said Piper under her breath.

Nina reached across Piper and retrieved her bag. She unbuttoned the pouch and pulled out the small blanket.

"Why are you calling me a creep?" Piper turned to face her friend and quietly muttered, "I wouldn't be in this mess if you'd been truthful about all the secrets from the very beginning. And it's all *your* fault."

"What!" Nina shook her head in disbelief. "Look, Piper, no one forced you to come down here. No one dragged you down the yueblion. If I recall, you came willingly."

"Yeah, but maybe I wouldn't have if you'd been honest with me. You lied to me about so many things. How can you be my best friend and be a li—"

"A what?" Nina leaned toward the accuser. "Listen, I've never lied to you. I've explained everything to you. I can't help it if you're so blind you just can't see the truth."

"The truth?"

"Yeah, the truth."

"Oh, just leave me alone," mumbled Piper.

Both girls turned away from one another in anger. Hearing parts of the quiet discord, Hodges turned his head while remaining watchful over the fading princess. He appeared in control, yet the beams from Edip's luminar disclosed an emergent distress in his deep eyes.

Exhaustion and despair had taken a heavy toll on Nina. Covering herself, she turned her tired eyes upward into the blackness. Her thoughts drifted. Part of her deeply regretted consenting to the rescue and telling Piper any of the secrets, but another part yearned to be a heroine and save the princess. Her scalp felt numb; her limbs tingled.

Rolling her head toward the dungeon door, she stared in quiet fascination at a faint light that emanated beyond the metal bars. Perched between two bars was a strange silhouette that resembled one of the creatures atop of the fortress. The black object remained still as if it were spying on the prisoners. Nina rubbed her eyes and took a second glance but the bird had vanished. She squinted again; the light behind the door grew brighter and swirled with gray textures. Oddly, she found herself standing on a bleak, distant shore. A figure, hovering between the twilight sky and shimmering sea, moved closer to the gray beach. Again, Nina rubbed her weary eyes in disbelief. How was this possible? Could it be? Yes, it was Arianna Angeliqué, the mysterious Wish-Weaver beckoning to her.

"Arianna, is that you? Have you come to help me?"

"Stay by the shore and do not venture out upon the waters."

"But I'm afraid. My friends and I are in trouble; one is about to die. Can you help us?"

The figure replied in echoing tones, "I am here not to render help but to deliver a message. Nina, search your heart and understand. Nothing you have received has been given arbitrarily or capriciously. All you have seen and learned is for a reason, guided by the hand of Providence."

The mystic form moved to the edge of the shore and stood face-to-face with her. Arianna's hand reached out and touched Nina's forehead.

"Remember!"

Suddenly Nina was in her bedroom. She moved to the window and peered out at the neighborhood. Stalks were tied to lampposts and pumpkins adorned the stoops. She turned the wall calendar above her desk. It was just before Halloween, last Halloween. Her thoughts were drawn to a stir on her bed. She backed up to the window, only to see herself awaking from a deep sleep. Amazed, she stood absolutely still to witness the incredible morning vision unfold.

The yawning girl sat up and brushed the open novel to one side. She sprang out of bed and twirled in front of the mirror. Nina watched the vision of herself begin her ballet warm-ups with a quick stretch, turnout, and allongé. Then came the demi-plié, dégagé, cisaeux, relevé, and cambré. Her feet were not changing positions fast enough for an entrechat quatre jump – her most difficult move.

After several minutes she danced back to the bed and resumed reading the novel from the night before. Nina heard her mother call from downstairs.

"Honey, it's about time to get up. Would you please straighten up your room a little before breakfast?"

"Okay, Mom."

"And remember you also need to practice your piano lesson sometime this morning as well."

Guilt squelched the enjoyment of reading for the moment. Breathing a deep sigh, Nina began the chore of tidying up the room. On her tall dresser lay an assortment of trinkets, stickers, 45-speed records, and fragrant lotions on either side of her mahogany jewelry box. As she arranged the items, she glanced in the mirror above her dresser to assess how much time it would take to fix her long hair the way she liked it. And if Piper were around to help, Nina would have preferred braids.

After peering into the mirror for the fourth time, something unusual caught her peripheral vision. At first she thought it was her imagination, for Nina's ability to contrive and pretend knew no limits. Standing motionless like a statue, she glanced at the Sea City lifeguard insignia on her baby blue T-shirt and then quickly jerked her hands in the air. Like Simon Says, the arms of her image followed her motion in almost perfect synchrony. But anything less than exact would be cause for suspicion.

Nina watched as her curious self examined the eyes of her reflection. Paralyzed with intrigue more than fear, she felt a creepy awareness come upon her, as if she were staring at another person.

"Are you me? Are you really me or are you someone else?" implored Nina, feeling somewhat foolish for asking such a ridiculous question.

The image imitated Nina's every movement with precision, which aggravated her all the more. Repeatedly she asked the image with more intensity and insistency.

Finally the reflection broke the mimicry. Its facial expression resembled Nina's when she had been caught committing some kind of infraction. Reluctantly, the reflection leaned into the mirror to whisper, "What I am doing is in direct violation of the regulations. Please do not tell anyone!"

Nina blinked. "How is this possible? How can you be real and live in there?"

"I am very much alive. But you must keep my existence a secret. Please, you must!"

"Oh, ah...your, your secret is safe with me," replied Nina in amazement. At first she could not believe this breach of reality. "Do you have a name?"

"My name is Kaleena."

"But how can this be?"

"Nina, I know this may be so strange to you, but I am really here – and very much alive."

Staring in disbelief, Nina moved closer to the glass. "What is it like in there?"

"Believe it or not, my world is very much like your own, save for some obvious differences that one would expect in a mirror-image dimension."

By the window Nina watched and relived the moments when she first encountered her image. Observing the conversation, she snickered to see her younger self asking what seemed like a thousand questions of the patient image.

"Is it like my world? I mean, do people live in there?"

"Yes, Nina. In the Looking Glass Realm people live very much like people in your world. However, images have the sworn duty to reflect, first and foremost."

"But it all seems so impossible!"

"Perhaps to you, but *my* world is as real as yours is. We exist in the same time but in another space," offered the image.

"Gosh, it really changes things – at least for me," said Nina.

"What do you mean?"

"I don't know. I guess how I see things and what I believe to be really true."

Leaning against the window sill, Nina listened to the vision of Kaleena describing her world. Kaleena told of how all images carry a secret device hidden on them called a reflectic-fractometer. The device informs all images where their counter image is and when or where to reflect back. Pulling up her left sleeve, Kaleena revealed a small electronic device strapped to her upper arm. Multicolored dots flashed from its corrugated surface. Kaleena divulged that the difficult aspect of the job was doing precisely what the person looking into the mirror was doing while looking just like that person. This took countless hours of practice and preparation in special institutions designed by the Optomital Continuum, the governmental overseers in the Looking Glass Realm.

"We sometimes ignore our duties though," confessed Kaleena.

"What do you mean?" Nina inquired.

"Sometimes images get just plain weary of their duties and will shirk reflecting in minor objects such as windows or other reflective, non-mirror surfaces. If people in your world paid more attention to it, they would soon discover this fact for themselves. As for me, I love reflecting for you, because you are so different and full of life."

Nina's eyes grew wider at the gracious compliment. "Kaleena, had I known about you, I would have tried to become your friend long ago. And to think of the million times I've stared at you totally unaware that you were right there staring back."

Both girls exchanged vacant stares followed by broad smiles and giggles.

"Yes, I know your face better than my own," Kaleena said. "I know so much about you too!"

In the vision Nina heard her mother call again from downstairs.

"Breakfast is ready! Come on down."

Kaleena leaned toward the glass and whispered, "If the Observers discover our secret, the consequences will be very unpleasant for me!"

"Who are they?" asked Nina.

"It would take too much time to tell you now; maybe I can explain the next time we encounter. We just have to be very careful," said the image with growing apprehension.

With that, Kaleena reached beyond the frame of the mirror. Nina stood motionless. Suddenly the very center of the mirror became distorted. Kaleena carefully extended her finger to the center of the disturbance. Instinctively, Nina reached out likewise. Their fingertips touched.

"Wow! This is so weird. What a feeling," Nina whispered.

Her image smiled. "Strange tingling on this side too."

Moments later Kaleena retracted her finger. The mirror rippled as she resumed reflecting for Nina.

Nina continued watching the vision of her younger self stealing glances back at the wondrous mirror before exiting.

The bedroom began to swirl; textures and color faded into gray. All was black until she realized that she was back on the foreign shore. Floating out to sea was the specter, whose pale shroud rustled in the gentle breeze.

"But what does it all mean? Arianna, why did you show me these things?" Nina shouted to the sea.

The silent figure moved on and disappeared beyond the mist. All was quiet save the gentle waters washing on the shifting sands and the beating of her heart.

Chapter Seventeen

Kaleena's Hand

Midnight

W hen her tired eyes opened, Nina saw the dungeon door. Looking about she noticed the gnomes and Piper lying on the cold ground; Hodges sat, attending to the waning princess.

"Hodges, what is to become of us?" she whispered. "How are we to escape from this place and carry Cirlaena back to the kingdom?"

The lanky scout rose. Careful not to step on the reclined gnomes, he slowly paced.

"It is a matter of what is to be. You see, dear Nina, Yurggie is part of the magnificent plan that transcends us five. Unbeknownst to the cannoid, he is fulfilling a piece of the grand design — a line, a thread in the beautiful tapestry of providential provision."

"Tapestry? What do you mean?" asked Nina.

The starling looked through the bars then turned to face the girl. "We are all part of the divine tapestry. You see, we often observe the side that resembles tangles, knots, and loose ends – a nondescript display of meaninglessness. But on the other side there is purpose and meaning – a beautiful design of the weaver's handiwork."

The others awakened to the wise words of the starling, who continued pacing in front of the dungeon door.

"What we have seen along our journey appears to us as a tumultuous series of events. However, like the tapestry, we must have faith that there is an Artist at work on the loom. And that is where we derive our strength and peace."

The girls stared in wonder at the scout, whose words tugged at their fragile souls. Hunger gnawed Nina's petite frame. With a wrinkle of her nose and a sniff, she reached into her knapsack to retrieve a morsel of the wrapped wafer.

"So you said that even Yurggie is part of the tapestry?" asked Nina.

"Precisely. After all, who watches the watchmen? You see, we rescuers need a rescuer of a different sort, and that is about to take place. I cannot tell you any of the details, but I can tell you that such actions demand sacrifice of the highest degree.

"Nina, Piper, are you both willing to make a sacrifice for another? Are you both willing to take a great risk? Moreover, are you both able to have another sacrifice for you that you might be saved?"

Nina's head hung low, for she was too tired to ponder these thoughts, which she perceived as another riddle. Her eyes moved to Piper, whose yawns were ready to succumb to the calls of sleep. Thoughts of home splashed upon Nina's mind. But those thoughts remained firmly suppressed by the weight of incarceration.

The word *sacrifice* oscillated in her weary mind. Was the sacrifice to involve them? What did Hodges mean? And were his words an omen? With that she slumped over and adjusted the pack as a pillow. Soon she joined Piper in a brief but artificial escape.

The giant, ravenous ravens did not notice the cannoid cleverly darting from among the strange stalagmites scattered about the northern boundary of Darkondusk. Yurggie was not a scout, but he had a keen sense of direction. Moving straight for the opening in the barrion, he disappeared in the dark tunnel. Once deep within, Yurggie bellowed a soft, peculiar moan again and again. Stopping to listen, he walked about as if expecting something unusual to happen. Suddenly from the dense darkness appeared a figure whose presence was felt beyond the five senses.

The Wish-Weaver reached down and quieted the animal with gentle strokes along its soft, furry underside.

"Now, now. I have been watching you all from afar. I sensed that you and your friends had entered Darkondusk some time ago. Why do you summon me at this hour? Am I to assume there is trouble for the Kimonos?" Arianna asked.

The cannoid responded in a grunting language unknown to Uplanders or gnomes, but the sounds triggered grave concern for the girl.

"Come, dear Yurggie. We must not delay, for the Kimonos is in danger and the princess is in great distress." She walked toward the exit with the most unusual expression on her beautiful face.

"I see that things are now unfolding in the manner that was described to me – things the Grand Patriarch foresaw. However, Feedunkulus promised me that no harm would befall the girls. I trust that he was correct in his assumption." It was unclear if her words were meant for the cannoid or if she were merely speaking to herself.

Arianna hastened to the castle with no thought of discovery, and the dreadful birds were oblivious to her presence. Yurggie frantically tried to keep pace while zigzagging through the rocky formations. Approaching the moat did not impede her swift pace. Once at the water's edge, she paused for the cannoid.

"Brave friend, you must walk as I," she whispered while waving her pale hands across his furry back.

They both marched across the surface of the still waters and entered the elongated crack in the cliff. Pausing to allow Yurggie to catch up, the numinous being reached in her blue dress and withdrew a small device that resembled a compass. She read the dials and then pocketed the thing. With Yurggie by her side, she moved deeper into the foreboding citadel.

The musty air within the cell hung heavy, making it more cumbersome to breathe. Hodges resumed his gentle caressing of Cirlaena's brown, matted hair that once graced her royal tiara. Time was now neither friend nor foe, for the gnomes and girls wearily waited for nothing, hoping for something. Deliverance seemed improbable at best.

The sound of light footsteps aroused Edip, who stood and approached the metal barrier. He leaned into the opening; the chilled bars stung his ears.

"Have you returned to wreak havoc upon us?" huffed Edip in anger.

"Hush. It is I, Arianna Angeliqué of the Jêhvahaér."

Pausing to assess the quiet announcement, the gnome tilted his head. The tall scout joined him at the bars.

"I do not know of you," said Hodges to the figure in the hall. "But I surmise that you shall play a role in our rescue."

The stunning Jêhvahaér peered into the cell and looked at the figures within. The subtle grunts of the cannoid told his master of the visitor's intentions.

"I have come to help you, but I am forbidden to interfere directly with your temporal affairs," said Arianna.

Hodges leaned forward, confronting the silhouette face-to-face. "If you cannot help us directly, then how can you assist at all?"

With those stark words still echoing in the corridor, Arianna looked about the hallway.

Hodges continued. "Can you not at least retract the staff that bars the door? The others cannot reach it, and I am unable to touch or levitate it. Are you permitted to at least lift the staff from the hooks?"

"No, Master Starling. As I said, I cannot interfere directly. I cannot release you from your imprisonment."

The scout turned his head to the others and sighed. "For whatever reason, it seems that plans have changed."

"Hodges, can't you just, just—" Nina caught herself from any further comment on the matter.

The scout returned to the princess. For the first time the others witnessed something different in their leader's countenance that was quite indefinable – impatience, annoyance, or perhaps a shadow of discouragement. Nina stood and moved toward the bars.

"Arianna, it is so good to see you again, although I must admit I didn't expect to see you here. Listen, there must be a way to help us. Please, you are powerful and wise. You must think of a way, or we will all surely die in this place!"

Tears streamed down Nina's face as she sobbed. Glancing to the left of the metal door, Arianna studied the hallway with extraordinary discernment and then stared back at Nina wide-eyed.

"I cannot help you directly. You must help yourself and your friends. Now think."

Nina frowned. "What can I do? We are stuck in here; there's no way out except through this door."

"Think!" implored the Jêhvahaér, whose patience seemed to be ebbing. "You have the answer within you. Deep down inside you lies the key. Search your thoughts!"

"But I can't." Tears flowed down Nina's reddened cheeks.

"Nina, do you remember?"

"Remember what?" Nina's expression suddenly changed as if she had just received an epiphany.

"Ah, ah – the beach? The vision?"

"Yes, the vision. Do you remember the vision?" asked Arianna.

Nina glanced at the others behind her and back at the visitor, whose stare had turned into a broad smile.

"Yes, now I think I know. Arianna, go down the hall to the mirrors – hurry!" Nina pointed to the right.

Nearly tripping over Yurggie, the Jêhvahaér darted down the corridor from where she had entered the prison. Grabbing one of the long mirrors from the wall, she carried it to the prisoners' cell and turned it on herself. She made no reflection, yet Yurggie's reflection danced at its base.

"Nina Leigh, come here to the door, quickly! And Piper, give her the light." Arianna said.

"Now what do I do?" asked Nina, holding the light with one hand and wiping her moistened cheeks with the other.

Arianna turned the mirror to face the door. "Stare at the mirror. Hold the light near the bars and look into the glass."

Nina obeyed, seeing only her tired, tousled reflection swaying from side to side.

"Look deeply," Arianna said.

Nina obeyed. "But nothing's happening." The others within the cell huddled about Nina as she stood statuesque.

"Look deeper. You must look deeply!"

Nina gazed at her reflection. Finally, after what seemed like hours, the image winked. "Kaleena!" she exclaimed.

The reflection looked about at the others surrounding Nina and then glanced from side to side.

Arianna peered from behind the mirror. "Speak to her, Nina. Request of her. She will listen."

Nina leaned toward the mirror. "Kaleena, we are perishing. We need your help. This evil ruler has us locked in this dungeon. Unless you can help us, I will die along with my friends. And you too will die along with me."

Kaleena's eyes saddened. "What do you wish me to do, Nina? Tell me and I will help."

"The staff that bars the door is out of our reach. But you can pull it loose and free us. Can you reach into my world and lift the staff?"

"Nina, you know I cannot enter your world. I exist within the mirror. If I leave it, I will fade."

"You don't have to leave the mirror. All you need to do is reach out with your hand – just your hand!"

"But it will begin to fade."

"Yes, but when you pull your arm back into the mirror it will be restored," offered Arianna.

Kaleena looked worried. She jittered nervously.

Nina pleaded again. "It'll take just a second to remove the staff. I know you can do it."

Kaleena knew the severe consequences of violating the Looking Glass Codes. "Nina, do you remember what I told you last year? If I am found out by the Observers, I could be erased, replaced by another."

"Kaleena, please. If you love me, you will help me."

The saddened face of the reflection lifted with a tender smile. Silently the image reached to the side of the frame to actuate the mirror. For a moment the aged surface of the glass rippled and glowed. Nina watched the slender hand she knew so well reach beyond the surface. Arianna moved the mirror closer to the door.

With modest effort, Kaleena lifted the long object from the rusty iron hooks that were affixed on each side of the metal doorframe. Quickly she retracted her hand; the mirror returned to its proper reflection.

"Now go, all of you. Escape while you can," said the Wish-Weaver as she leaned the mirror against the moldy wall.

The tyranny of the moment made no allowance for remarks of gratitude. The Kimonos fled, with the starling carrying the waning princess. Arianna bent over and smiled into the empty mirror.

"How clever of you," she whispered before vanishing from the desolate dungeon.

Chapter Eighteen

The Piper's Tune

Thursday, April 22 (after midnight)

Down the deserted corridor the Kimonos hurried with the scout's outstretched luminar leading the way. Yurggie and the gnomes strode briskly behind, followed by Piper and then Nina in the rear. Nina so wished to settle the matter with her best friend, for the tension between them was quite apparent. Why wouldn't Piper just recant and forgive? Why the ongoing grudge even through the tempestuous trials of their incredible journey. Her gaze vacillated between Piper's heels and the light up ahead. The last thing she wanted to do at this point was stumble into the pouter and have to apologize for something so minor.

Sounds of shuffling shoes and rustling clothes filled the stillness as the team made their way to the stone stairway that led to the lower levels of the fortress.

"The descent ahead is slippery, so please be careful – and keep up the pace. We must flee in all due haste," whispered the starling.

In her mind Piper debated whether she should turn to check on her friend. However, selfish pride insisted that it was Nina's responsibility to ask Piper how she was faring.

After all, was it not Nina who had withheld so many secrets? Was it not Nina who had invited her to participate in the perilous rescue? And what kind of a best friend would place another friend in harm's way over and over again? Piper ruminated about these matters and would only succumb to illogic forged by an unforgiving spirit. After all, admission of any wrongdoing on her part would only lead to self-incrimination. For now her stubbornness would yield no such confession.

Yet Piper wrestled with the notion that behind her walked her closest friend. Behind her was the one who brought luster and even magic into her life. It was Nina who stood by her through all the good and bad times. Even when she was taunted by the school's biggest bullies, Dawn and Domino, Nina was the only one who ran to her defense.

She could not resist any longer. Piper turned to check on Nina.

"Hodges – she's gone! Nina's gone!" cried Piper.

The starling froze in his tracks and spun around. His deep eyes pried into the dark recesses of the passageway.

Grabbing Piper by the shoulder, he lowered his face with absolute sternness. His eyes widened. "When did you last see her? Tell me everything!"

"I – I saw her a while back."

"How far back?"

"I don't know – maybe about five minutes ago? But, but after that I kept my eyes on you all in front on me."

"Did you hear her walking behind you?" asked Hodges, glaring about at the uneven walls.

"Not really. Oh, I don't know," gasped Piper in utter fear.

"Hmm. All of you follow me – quickly now!"

The starling handed the fading princess to Edip and quickly backtracked. The others followed in tight formation. Yurggie lunged forward to catch up with his master, but Enver's sudden tugs on the leash kept the cannoid at bay.

On and on Hodges raced down the tunnel, stopping at every crevice and fissure. But all shadows were empty.

"She must have been captured by one of the guards. She cannot be far away," blurted the scout while zigzagging through the dark channel.

"But I saw nothing," replied Edip, panting to catch his breath and trying to balance the dying princess on his broad shoulder.

"I saw nothing as well," said Enver, yanking back on the leash. "How could someone have taken her so quietly?"

Agony swept over their spirits as each team member desperately searched for any clue to Nina's whereabouts. Tears trickled down Piper's reddened cheeks. How small the conflict seemed now that her friend was taken away. Guilt flooded her emotions; she felt ill.

Several yards ahead the starling stopped, as if to listen for some faint cry for help. The others huddled behind him.

Turning, he whispered, "Someone or something is to the right of us – inside the cleft. I will enter first. Stay close behind."

The starling led the team through the large breech in the rock. Cautiously they entered till the narrow pass opened to an irregular cavern. The darkness was stifling and enveloped the luminar's rays. Deep within the cave they gathered. All was silent until the fiend released a heavy snort. From across the enclosure lime-green orbs peered through the shadows.

"It appears that you all have left some things behind," grunted the beast, who held Nina by the mouth with his dreadful claw. Even the obscure light could not conceal the guard's hideous features.

Hodges stepped forward. "You cannot thwart our escape, kandalarian."

"You are mistaken, starling. I already have."

"I am warning you, release the girl now!" Hodges insisted.

As he moved forward the beast revealed what he clutched in the other hand.

"Move no closer or I will..."

"You know not what you possess," said Hodges.

"Oh *really?*" growled the beast with his guttural voice. "By the power of this magical staff, I command you to fall back!"

In amazement the others watched while their leader quickly obeyed and joined them against the far wall. Nina watched in horror, squirming to free herself; but it was of no use. Whimpering, she could only witness what seemed to be the final act of the unfolding nightmare.

"Ha! My master will be quite pleased when I report the news – that I alone captured the fleeing prisoners. Oh, this will bring me such glory – perhaps even the adjutancy." The kandalarian chortled and moved toward the narrow entrance. "And now I must leave you to your doom."

"You will not get away with this!" shouted an enraged Enver.

"It looks like I already have, you puny, pitiful thing. I shall bar the passage with the staff of power so that you cannot leave."

As he reached to lay the staff diagonally across the narrows, he stopped momentarily. Scanning the room, he barked, "Where is the other female?"

Suddenly, screaming filled the cave, catching the beast off guard. From the crevice Piper charged the kandalarian, snatching the staff away from him. Tumbling toward the others, she tossed the staff and yelled, "Hodges!"

The starling caught the artifact and quickly subdued the guard; the others leaped to Nina's side. The girls hugged and sobbed while the starling muscled the beast to the far side of the enclosure.

"Quick, everyone to the main passageway. And hurry!" ordered the leader.

"It is a matter of time until you are captured. There is no escaping Darkondusk," groused the brute, inching his way toward the others. "We will find you. You will never get past the moat."

"We shall see about that," mocked the starling as he leaned the staff to block the way. "Now it is *I* who command the Staff of Sandoval. It is I who ensnare you, foul wretch." The staff illuminated for a brief moment while the Kimonos fled.

Scurrying down toward the stairway, the team followed the scout's light. For obvious reasons Enver now took up the rear. In single file the girls could not face each other. Nonetheless, they could not contain their emotions any longer.

"Nina, I was so scared. I'm so, so glad you're safe and all right."

Nina smiled. "Thanks, Piper. Gosh, I can't believe you actually charged that monster. That was unbelievable!"

"Hush!" admonished the leader as they began their descent. "No more talking until we leave this miserable land."

Hodges took the princess from Edip's arms and continued on. Words were not necessary for that which needed to occur. The girls' relationship was finally on the mend, but uncertainty of what lay ahead consumed their thoughts.

Chapter Nineteen

Fears in Flight

Thursday, April 22 (early morning)

Grotesque claws thrusted upward; parchments scattered in the air. Some papers landed in the stagnant pool at the very center of the immense courtyard. The swing of the ruler's long, imperial coat was followed by laughter that ricocheted off the towering walls surrounding the beastly minions. The adjutant followed with a sickening cackle that mimicked a Halloween witch.

"To Hades with the agreement! I am not bound by a contract," boasted Borok.

The adjutant Bumpus laughed. "Yes, master, who needs the trolls? After all, you have kicked the gnomes where it hurts – you have stabbed them in the heart. In a little while they will surrender to your demands. And Shaptillicus will be forced to relinquish that which is rightfully yours."

Bumpus paused in quiet reflection. "Too bad the gnome king did not yield to the ransom's demands while he had the chance. So sad that it comes to this."

"Comes to this? Oh, you underestimate my diabolic plans, Bumpus."

"Oh, master, I know you are wise and will be the victor, but I thought that—"

"How confident you are, my malevolent mushroom," Borok said with a condescending air. "However, our arrogance must be tempered with wisdom lest we forget our true mission. Soon the weak, worthless Tréfon will feel excruciating pain when he learns of the failed rescue and death of his dullard daughter.

"Despair will give way to anger. With righteous indignation he will strike westward against his enemy, for he knows far too well that Shaptillicus is the grand architect of his daughter's misfortunes. Ah, I can see it now. Ill-prepared and unsuspecting, the king will send his gnome battalions into the great schism to retaliate against the trolls. Little does he know that his army is entering a trap."

"And that will bring the collapse of the gnomes' kingdom?" Bumpus inquired with an evil grin.

"On the contrary, my fiendish assistant. As much as I hate to admit it, the gnomes are capable warriors. But while they engage in battle with the trolls and goblins, our legions will emerge through the pass from the Bedloe Abidion. We shall enter the empire and launch our offensive strike against them all."

"But what of the bedloe? Will they just allow you to march through their lands?"

"Why, yes. You see, I have promised the spinners something irresistible."

"What, my lord?"

"That is my affair!" yelled Borok with a rumble. Restraining himself, he continued with a pleased expression. "Oh, the sequence of events is falling into our hands like a ripened dillonrod fruit. Can you not see how truly devilish this is? Soon the river and rich valley will be mine. Thereafter, my boot will rest on the heads of Shaptillicus, Orgetarex, and that weak-minded gozzi, Areovistus."

"But, master, how can we wage war against so many?"

The dark lord turned to his adjutant with an insidious grin. "Through their weaknesses we are made stronger." But he caught himself, for he did not wish to reveal the entire plan to anyone yet, including his heavy henchman.

"Ah, you are wise, master," praised Bumpus, turning to the mass in the square. "Hail to Darkondusk! All hail to Lord Borok!" The passionate words inspired the minions encircling the two. Grunts and groans heightened to screeches and howls. With a haughty and contemptuous spirit, Borok climbed upon the boulder that glowed with a tint of purple-gray in the gloaming's illumination.

The monstrous birds leaped from their high perches and circled overhead to pay homage to their conniving principal. So filled with himself was he that the dark lord barely noticed the giant ravens abandoning their strange ritual as they flew northward toward a ruse.

Borok's scornful eyes shifted to study the remnant in flight. His contorted face disclosed surprise and outrage to the onlookers.

"What is this?" he said.

"Why, it is nothing but the vordalics patrolling Darkondusk," offered Bumpus.

"No, you fool! Look again. Something is wrong!"

Bumpus cast his gaze toward the northern sky. "It is a strange thing..."

"It cannot be. It is impossible!" roared Borok.

"What is it, master? What troubles you?"

"It is the prisoners; they are escaping. All of you! Quick! To the northern gates and beyond. Away with you!"

Bumpus swiftly led the pack toward the broad wooden doors, which opened without effort of mechanical means. Borok leaped upon his ferocious wolfen and rode on, leading the mob across the drawbridge to follow the flock of foul creatures in the distance. Suddenly a brilliant light flashed across the shallow sky. Like thick black rain, the flapping creatures fell dead to the ground.

Borok spewed unthinkable profanities and shook with rage. "Curses! That starling has killed my vordalics. I will crush him and his friends for this atrocity." He swung his fists high in the air.

The girls could hardly keep up with the scout, who now bore the burden of carrying the dying princess over his shoulder. Nina peered back to see the fallen carcasses scattered behind, creating a gruesome cemetery of evil. The clamor of the distant hordes sent terror into the girls, for they knew that those who chased them would fancy no thought of survivors. No, this was a run for life, the last desperate hour of the relentless nightmare that haunted each step of their escape.

The scout moved them along through subtle inspiration. Faith in his wisdom and powers strengthened their hearts as they approached the irregular opening of the barrion. Without turning his head or altering his pace, the starling admonished the Kimonos with his deep, resounding tone.

"Keep running quickly through the passage. Gnomes, activate your luminars! Edip, take the lead; Enver take the rear. Once outside the channel we must take a shortcut through the petrified glades. We will hug the Southern Barrion till we reach the Great Telexian Divide. At that point I will confound the enemy but for awhile."

Piper whispered to Nina between quick breaths. "What does he mean by confounding the enemy?"

The starling interrupted, "My words speak of truth – of what is to come. My essence will blind those pursuing us; in a little while you shall see them no more."

The riddle did not placate their anxious minds, so Piper and Nina continued to follow the scout, pondering the meaning of his prophetic announcement. And even though the horror of being captured or killed plagued their thoughts, each step brought them closer to the journey's end. Yes, it would be the end – one way or another.

As they exited the tunnel, the starling took the lead once more. The gnomes craned their necks trying to scan the rocky ceiling for the hungry worms. Meanwhile, Hodges raised his palm upward. Radiant beams flooded the ceiling.

"I have no time to deal with these despicable parasites," he said.

Nina rushed forward and tapped the starling on the shoulder. "Why didn't you do that before?"

Hodges pressed onward and ignored the question, for the others would not understand why he had to restrain from overusing his powers.

Skimming the barrion, the team set their bearings to the east – to the mother of all barrions. Winding from south to north, the Great Telexian Divide lay west of and parallel to the Atlantic seaboard. Telexian provided a natural, impregnable barricade between the lands of good and evil. All but the scout and his cannoid knew they were heading into a dead-end, a vulnerable and indefensible position. But faith in Hodges brought a peace that somehow and some way their safety would be assured through the fiery ordeal.

The noise reached a crescendo from behind; they turned their heads. Pouring out of the pass and into the petrified glades were the tracking minions, led by Borok and Bumpus astride their dreadful beasts. The faint but distinctive shouts of Bumpus rose above the babble of the mob.

"Master, there they are, heading toward the great wall! They will be trapped!"

"Excellent! We will slay them against the rocks. And the starling will be the first to feel the slice of my blade!"

The murderous mass heightened their cries for revenge. Darkness seemed to flood the glades at the presence of such evil. Suddenly, several of the attackers danced about as if ordered to perform some strange jig. Others fell to the hardened ground, brushing their heads and faces in torment. Like an April shower the boreworms fell upon kandalarian brigades, dispersing the formations with panic and confusion.

Turning to his marauders, Borok yelled, "Onward! Forward! Leave the lame and dying, and follow me now!"

"But, master, what shall we do with the…"

"You insolent fool!" cried Borok. "March on or die!"

Those not bitten followed their leader on foot with renewed intention. The gap between the rescuers and the attackers narrowed with every second. The Kimonos hid behind a cluster of boulders, but the maneuver could not conceal their whereabouts for long.

Handing the princess to Edip, Hodges huddled the team together, almost as if he were suddenly altering the plans.

"I have no time for details, but you will do exactly what I say. I will leave you now so that you may escape. Do not worry for me; my destiny is secure."

"But why can't you come with us?" implored Nina.

"Yes, you must come with us, Hodges!" insisted Piper.

143

Ignoring their pleas, the starling turned to the steep precipice and placed his hand upon an etched design within the rock; the symbols glowed. The wall vertically split aside, leaving a small opening in the divide.

"Now go inside. To your left you will find graviton pads. Untie the devices and sit upon them. Keep your head and limbs tucked together as much as possible. The Paddox Passage lies within a magnetic anomaly, which will take you directly to the Southern Barrion of the First Kingdom. At the tunnel's end you will find an obvious device to open a hidden panel that will lead you to the Zander Zee."

"But you and Yurggie must come with us!" Nina cried, for she clearly discerned the consequence of his being left behind.

"No time for words. Now leave your lights behind. Quickly, inside! And remember the sacrifice that a friend has made for his friends at this very hour. Go now!" commanded Hodges with restrained tears in his eyes.

As his words ended, he spun around to the commotion behind him. The gnomes and girls swiftly ducked, entered the cave, and dropped their luminars along the inner walls.

Finding the pads, they followed Hodges' instructions. Facing the floating pads northward, the team grabbed their gear, sat on the pads, and gripped the side handles. As the opening gradually closed, Nina turned to witness the hostile hordes rounding the huge boulders. Immediately, the mysterious master scout flung off his long trench coat, unfolding what appeared to be a huge set of white wings, which arched upward and toward the attackers. Brilliant light emanated from his essence, blinding the menacing kandalarians. Shrills and shrieks resounded. The entrance closed.

The pads sent the team flying through the pitch-black corridor. The rush of stale air and the wobble of the humming devices were the only indicators of their speedy escape.

"How are you all doing?" yelled Edip, who sat in the front pad with the princess curled up in his husky arms.

"Forget us. How is Princess Cirlaena?" asked Nina.

"Fading – she is fading fast," Edip called back.

"What happened to Hodges? What will become of him? And Yurggie?" Piper cried.

"We have no answers to your questions, my dear friend. We only have each other and this present darkness to guide us to the light," offered Enver.

A sadness they had never known before invaded their hearts. Despair clouded any thought of escape. How could their safety be measured by the loss of their guardian, guide, and stay? Nina pondered all of this in silence. Extending her hands, she felt the rapid bumping of her fingertips, a telltale sign of their undetermined velocity and waning innocence.

"Wake up! Princess, please wake up!" came the shouts of Edip, who struggled to stir Cirlaena from slipping into unconsciousness. "I fear that I am losing her. Her breath grows shallow. She is so still."

Swishing air and broken spirits precluded further conservation. Time was running out; hope was all but gone. The Kimonos had bought their escape with many tears. And from their lips, fervent prayers rose silently like the censer's smoke from a sacred oblation.

Chapter Twenty

The Healing Waters

Later that same morning

With rusty chains Enver secured the graviton pads to eyelets on the interior wall. The devices fluttered and hovered inches apart from one another. He slipped outside the exit to scan the meadow for the others. Once he spotted the team, he actuated the small knob near the opening in the barrion. The small fissure slammed shut behind him.

Enver scurried down the slope toward the river and knelt beside Nina and Piper. The princess was reclined on her back along the bank. Edip dipped his cupped hand into the pure spring waters, which bubbled at the barrion's base like a slow-motion whirlpool. Carefully and patiently, the gnome sprinkled life-giving droplets onto the lips of the despondent princess.

"Edip, do you think she'll make it? Did we get back in time?" asked Nina, besieged with worry.

Piper rested next to her best friend; they held each other in fear of what seemed inevitable. So engrossed with the princess' well-being were they that the girls were oblivious to the beautiful landscape surrounding them.

"I do not know; it is too soon to tell. We must trust in the waters of promise and be patient. That is truly all we can do at this point, my friend."

Enver stood and waddled about the bank. "Edip, let us take a few of these fallen tamaracks by the rocks and tie them together with zadia vines. It will not be much of a raft, but the current will carry us northward to Tangelee."

The girls leaped forward to assist the stout gnome in gathering several small logs, which were much lighter than they appeared. Once the beams were laid side by side near the river's edge, Enver instructed the girls to steady the logs while he wove the thick, supple vines around the ends. Nina wondered if the makeshift raft could actually float, let alone carry them up the meandering river. Enver's encouraging words finally convinced her otherwise.

After nearly half an hour, Enver stood and called for Edip. "I think it is ready for us. Come bring the princess. We will keep the boat stable while you climb on with Her Majesty."

Edip awkwardly rose with the girl in his arms and made his way onto the raft. The others climbed aboard. Cool ripples rolled across the timbers, wetting the riders' pant legs and shoes. Envisioning the ending to their long, arduous journey, the weary travelers welcomed the chilly but refreshing waters of the Zander Zee.

The soft, splashing sounds were soothing. Piper felt compelled to say something. "It's hard to believe that we have traveled so far and done so much in just a few days. I bet the kids at school will sure be shocked when we tell them about all we've seen down here."

Tempted to snap a response, Nina paused and tempered her words. "Piper, unfortunately we will not be able to share any of this with those in our world. You too are now sworn to absolute secrecy."

"Yes, Piper," reproved Edip. "You cannot breathe a word of Gilacia, for uplanders would come upon us with insatiable curiosities and ruin all that we have and love. No, my dear Piper, we need you to be quite silent on this matter – forever!"

Piper cast her gaze downward to the moistened deck. "I would never wish anything bad to happen to you all down here, especially to the gnome kingdom and the starlings. I promise you now that I will hold all of this a secret for good, once, and for all – cross my heart and hope to...!"

The others' affirming grins sealed the oath. The diminished Kimonos studied the landscape as the raft steadily moved northward by the currents of the mighty Zander Zee. The girls soaked in the scenes, knowing that it might be quite some time before they could enjoy the extraordinary, provincial beauty of the kingdom again.

Piper turned to Nina; their eyes met. "Uh, Nina, I would like to..."

"Not now," came the reply and a warm smile.

"But all I wanted to do was to—"

"Wait till be get to Palmyra," said Nina, pulling off her sneakers and soggy socks. She turned about and slipped her feet into the cool waters.

"Ah, that feels so good," she whispered.

Enver continued to poke the long pole into the river, guiding the raft through the curves and bends along the way. If not for their exhausted state and the condition of the princess, the river ride would have been quite pleasant. While most mysteries had been disclosed along the way, two unanswered affairs rested solely upon each member's mind. What had become of their guide and his faithful cannoid? Would the rescued one survive? And with each slight movement of Cirlaena's hands and feet, hope kept a watchful gaze northward.

The rickety raft continued drifting with the current. To the west Nina saw the rooftops of Posha and then Pro-coak Toanday. Turning her head, she looked upriver. Ahead, she saw the tall spires and towers of Gnomen City. The white granite steps of Palmyra Pavilion seemed so tiny but beckoned to her heartstrings like an alluring enchantress. Adjacent to the golden entertainment center was gorgeous Tangelee, with its pristine waters that played upon Palmyra's monumental stairway.

Near the widening of the river, Piper was the first to catch a glimpse of the Royal Palace and Spoleo Hall, which signified the long-awaited respite. On the banks near Palmyra stood a lone figure that spotted the travelers and then darted out of sight. As the Kimonos approached the grand cloisters and white marble stairs, a small crowd gathered to witness the landing of the makeshift vessel.

"It is the rescue team! It is Princess Cirlaena and the others!" shouted a voice among the diminutive people, who burst into rounds of cheers that filled Palmyra's frescoed walls.

Several guards hurried down the huge steps to the dock. The weary travelers were helped off the waterlogged platform. Several other gnomes appeared with a stretcher and carried the princess up the steps and out of sight. Nina, Piper, Enver, and Edip were escorted up to the Pavilion's terrace, which wrapped the outer columns along the lakeside. Embraces abounded; congratulations filled the air. Nina and Piper were overwhelmed by the adoration of the growing throng. To the right near a great Corinthian column, Nina saw a familiar figure that drew near to her.

"Welcome home, my dear brave Miss Fithian. And well done. You have performed with amazing valor, both you and Miss Slack," said Grand Patriarch Feedunkulus with a broad stately smile.

Nina reached back and grabbed Piper by the arm, pulling her to the patriarch. "Sir, I couldn't have done anything without Piper Rae. Along with Enver and Edip, she was my strength the whole way."

Piper blushed and gazed down at her wet feet. "Yep, I was sure a big help," she quipped. Nina giggled.

"It has been quite some time since I have seen such faith and courage. I deeply commend you both. And I am sure the king will be very pleased as well," said the elderly statesman, who turned and vanished behind the column.

The girls rejoined Edip and Enver, who were surrounded by friends and admirers asking thousands of questions about the rescue. As Nina heard Edip offer snippets of the adventures, she turned her eyes to the crystalline lake and lost her thoughts in its grace. The gloaming's everlasting rays struck the surface, creating a sparkling display like lustrous diamonds. So many trials, so many hours, and so many fears. Yet Nina had overcome them all through an inner strength and the unyielding friendships of her beloved friends. How striking was the gain! How rewarding was this gift!

"Nina, is this a good time?" asked Piper.

Nina smiled and took her friend's hand. They walked to the edge of the massive stairs. Piper looked down at the small raft being towed away.

"I just wanted to apologize being such a big baby."

Nina smiled. "Oh, it's okay…"

Piper's eyes welled up with tears. "Wait! I have to finish. I now know why you couldn't tell me any of the secrets. Others trusted in you not to say a word. And, and instead of being an understanding friend, I acted like, like a creep. Will you please forgive me?"

Nina grabbed her friend in a sisterly embrace. "Of course I forgive you. You are my best friend forever."

Tears streamed down their faces. A soft tap on their shoulders pulled them apart.

"Girls, what of Princess Cirlaena? Is she all right?" asked a little gnome girl in a frumpy oversized dress.

Nina grinned. "I'm not sure, but let's go see how the princess is doing."

Nina motioned to Piper; the trio walked hand-in-hand through the magnificent theatre of Palmyra. Moving up the center aisle of the structure, Nina turned her head to steal a glance at the stage on which she had performed last June. Pleasant thoughts cascaded through her mind. She reflected on the standing ovation rendered by the crowd, who marveled at her ballet repertoire. How she missed those delicate movements and that splendid moment in time. However, the resolute grip of reality turned her head to another crowd that stood in loose formation beyond the last rows.

Chapter Twenty-One

Beyond the Brink

Thursday, April 22 (afternoon)

S tanding outside the great wooden doors of majestic Spoleo Hall, the girls could not distinguish which seemed more urgent: waiting for news of the princess or wanting to return home. Nina glanced through the mingling crowd to observe what her two gnome friends were doing. However, they had disappeared from sight.

A stout official dressed in military apparel approached the two disheveled onlookers.

"Miss Fithian, Miss Slack, allow me to introduce myself. I am Lieutenant General Eeleeg Rokáhn. Would you both do me the honor of following me into Spoleo Hall? Those inside wish to see you immediately."

Nina and Piper followed Rokáhn to the far side of the great building where the right panel of two brass doors was partially open. As the lieutenant general swung the panel inward, the girls beheld the large oval gopherwood table they had seen days earlier. At the table's head sat the king with the same individuals who were at the briefing Monday afternoon. King Tréfon slowly stood to honor the heroines. The entourage followed the king's lead. Rokáhn shut the door.

"Ah, come in, brave souls, and be seated."

The girls reluctantly moved toward the stately brass chairs at the end of the table. Dawdling, they sat and looked at Edip, Enver, and the other smiling faces of the diminutives.

"As king, it is my pleasure to extend to both of you our sincere appreciation for your valiance in the safe return of my daughter. Words cannot adequately express my joy and pleasure. Both of you are to receive our deepest commendations as true heroes to my people in the First Kingdom. For this I ask you both to remain with us for just one more hour, for we have planned a special presentation of Princess Cirlaena to the citizens of Gnomen City. Would you please honor us with your extended presence?"

Nina and Piper looked at each other, studying one another's face. Nina turned to the king.

"Your Majesty, on behalf of my dearest friend, Piper Rae Slack, and myself, we would love to stay. But we must leave shortly afterwards, because I feel that trouble is waiting for us up in our neighborhood."

"You can say that again," murmured Piper.

Conversations filled the spacious conference room, but the king empathized with the girls' situation. He raised his hand to quiet the others.

"I surely understand, Miss Fithian. No sense to worry your parents." Looking down at his wrist, he announced, "Let us not further delay what needs to be done. Let us proceed to the Court of Honors."

The king rose and exited through the interior pocket doors behind him. The girls and others quietly left through another door. Down a long, torch-lit corridor the entourage walked with the four friends engaged in small talk about the incredible rescue of the princess and the sudden disappearance of the starling.

The doorway ahead swung open to a massive courtyard where a great chattering mass of witnesses had gathered in front of a white marble stage. Nina and Piper stood frozen at the doorway, afraid to step out into the spotlight with the other dignitaries.

Edip leaned toward the girls. "They have gathered to welcome Princess Cirlaena, you know. But moreover they have come to honor two courageous girls."

Nina and Piper raised their brows, breathed deeply, and stepped out to meet the throng of admirers. A thunderous applause erupted. On the stage a purple curtain was lifted, revealing the king and his queen standing side by side in their royal attire. Chants of joy rang out as the royal couple stepped forward. The applause was nearly deafening to Piper, who held her ears to muffle the clamor.

Quieting the crowd with his hands, King Tréfon stepped forward to join the girls and their two gnome companions.

"There are days that mark history, and there are days that make history. The Kimonos has done remarkably well – and ultimately changed the course of our destiny. We are indebted to these four rescuers as well as to our allies of the Starling Sphere.

"And now to Edip and Enver, I bestow the honor of Guardians, Protectors of the Crown. And to Miss Nina Leigh Fithian and Miss Piper Rae Slack, I extend the great honor of High Citizens of the Kingdom. My fellow gnomes, we owe our eternal gratitude to these heirs of victory!"

As the king offered the jeweled medallions, the crowd launched into revelry. Small fireworks filled the shallow sky with sparkling bursts of color. The girls hugged the king, queen, and honorable officials beside them. Nina looked to the side of the platform to see Grand Patriarch Feedunkulus offering his approval through a wink and a slight bow.

Suddenly trumpets heralded a sweet announcement, and all eyes moved to the granite staircase at the far side of the stage. Cirlaena appeared at the top and gracefully descended to the cheers of the multitude. The monarch was tempted to quiet the clamor for a proper protocol, but the occasion dictated otherwise.

"Piper, she looks so beautiful, so lovely in her gorgeous gown," said Nina, who pondered how Cirlaena appeared much more human than gnomen.

"I can't believe how quickly she's gotten better," Piper replied.

While the applause continued, Edip leaned toward the girls. "She has been restored by the waters of Zander Zee. Remember what Hodges said about the river?"

"Kinda," awkwardly admitted Piper.

"Well, after receiving the staff of power, Arch Sandoval blessed the river in the name of the gift-giver. But as in all things, such as coins, there are two sides to view. The waters bring blessings of life abundant and longevity, yet the waters also bind us to the source. You see, prolonged distance from the waters brings certain death to all gnomes in this land."

He breathed deeply and continued. "Girls, my people are bound by and to the river for both protection and dependence of life. And it is the numinous power of the Zander Zee that the trolls and their evil allies desire to possess and control. This is precisely why they wish to destroy us. They desire what the waters offer. Today you have witnessed the river's healing powers with your own eyes. Now, behold *your* princess."

Without hesitation and much to everyone's surprise, the glowing princess walked straight through the assembled dignitaries to the girls. The multitude of spectators quieted.

"Nina, Piper, thank you for risking your lives to save mine. Your courage filled me with strength to make the journey back home. I can never repay you. All that I have is yours—now and always."

In sincere gratitude the princess leaned forward with a royal curtsy. The crowd cheered, chanting:

All hail to Princess Cirlaena,
the next regent and queen of the First Kingdom.

The king escorted Her Majesty offstage to meet the waiting subjects below. Meanwhile, Viceroy Ober and Generals Dalandúshae and Shäbáhn congratulated the pair and joined the king offstage. Lieutenant General Rokáhn made his way through the waning gathering to offer his praise as well.

"I commend you both on your gallant mission," he said.

Nina smiled, pulled Piper to her side, and replied, "Well, when you have great team members, you can do almost anything."

Rokáhn gave a peculiar grin. "Yes. You did well. Perhaps too well."

With that he turned on his heels and walked away. The girls stared at each other, trying to deny some hidden meaning in his words. A tap on the shoulder caught Nina's attention. She turned and gazed into the eyes of wisdom.

"Good day, girls," greeted the venerable Grand Patriarch. "Piper, would you be so kind as to deliver these papers to Edip? And tell him that I need to see the report about the Royal Diadem as soon as possible."

Piper smiled. "Of course. Where is he?"

"He is standing behind that crowd down by SheeNao Depot."

After he explained the way to the commerce center, Piper took the folder from his wrinkled hand and hurried down the cobblestone street.

The statesman turned to Nina, who knew that her friend's errand was merely a diversion so that more serious matters could be discussed in private.

"Many unanswered questions gnaw at your heart, Miss Fithian. You have seen visions of wonder while others have chosen a lesser view. Tell me, do you understand what you have experienced in recent days?"

Nina's expression changed as perplexity clouded her thoughts. Her bright hazel eyes looked into his.

"I thought I understood, but I guess I don't."

Feedunkulus smiled. "It is wise to admit one's shortcomings. To many it is the first step to wisdom and understanding. Tell me your thoughts – your doubts."

With tearing eyes, she spoke. "What of Hodges? Is he dead? Did those animals kill him?"

"What do you think?"

"He *must* have died. How could he escape from their attack? There were hundreds, thousands of those kandalarians against him. How could he have had a chance? Sir, you know things...you can see things. Can you tell me if he's still alive?"

The Grand Patriarch reached for Nina's hand. "You are correct. I can see many things. However, my young friend, even the most wise and gifted are not privy to all matters."

Nina glanced around and turned again to the elder; her face reddened. "But don't you even have a clue what happened to him?"

"I cannot tell you that which I do not know."

Nina pulled her hand away and walked toward the crowd a few feet before returning to the old gnome.

"Then tell me this," she said in an angry tone, "why did we have to go through all that misery, miles and miles of needless misery, when all we had to do was enter that secret passage into the big divide and ride those floating cushion things to the castle and back? If we'd done that, we could've avoided all this stupid, stupid stuff, and Hodges probably wouldn't have died! We wasted so much time when we could have—"

"Nina, Nina, it had to be that way!" Feedunkulus said. "What you call stupid and a waste of time was necessary."

"But why?" she sobbed, drawing the attention of bystanders.

Taking her by the hand again, the elderly patriarch walked her to a nearby garden. His eyes met hers.

"A shortcut would have failed. You see, it was the journey that made the difference. Each mile, each trial made changes – in you. Valor was strengthened through the risks. Your faith was made perfect in the face of fear. Nina, you are *not* the same person you were a week ago. You have changed, and for the better. And your friend? Piper Slack is all the stronger because of you. This is why you *both* were chosen. It is that decision which made the mission a success."

Nina wiped her tears away. "But Hodges is gone – he's gone!"

"And your friends and the princess are safe, and for that we can be thankful."

She gazed at the teal-colored blossoms in the garden. "But I feel so empty," she said softly.

"I am sure you do," replied the Grand Patriarch, "but you are part of a much bigger plan. Nina, think about this. Arianna's revelations and all the adventures were given for a reason. And this is not the end but the beginning. Even greater adventures lie ahead for you and your friends."

"Friends?"

"Yes, Nina – friends."

Nina gazed into his beaming eyes. "And you...you know this?"

"I see this."

The dark tunnel that led to the yueblion seemed like another leg of their mission. Fears of morbidity and mortality had vanished. But another fear confronted the girls.

"Edip, I'm afraid to go home. If my parents have found out that I was gone, my goose is cooked," said Nina.

Piper jumped in. "Yeah, my folks will kill me if they know I've been gone so long."

"Do not worry. The deceleron has done its work. Besides, while we were on the mission, the general had scouts watch the activities in both your homes. To date all is well," Edip said.

As they neared the chamber at the base of the great shaft, Nina turned to her stout bearded friend. "One thing is for sure. I can't wait to get out of these clothes and these soggy socks and sneakers."

"Yeah, me too," added Piper. "I wish we could've brought more of our stuff down here, but we had plenty to carry as it was."

Piper looked up the metal and stone steps. "And the thought of lugging our packs up the yueblion – well, I just don't think I have the energy."

Edip smiled. "Why not leave them down here? I'll have some scouts bring them up to the tree later this evening."

Finally, Nina and Edip embraced to say their farewells.

"Edip, do you think that the generals will find out how the princess was really kidnapped?" asked Nina with tears in her eyes.

"I have faith that they will, and soon. I know that Enver is working with the officials on the case," replied Edip.

"Oh, that's good. And be sure to give Enver another hug for us. I miss him already," said Nina lowering her head. "And, Edip, always remember that I love you."

"I love you too – the both of you," replied the gnome.

Piper leaped into the embrace, sobbing.

"Now, now. It is time for you both to go home," Edip said with sadness. "Go now and enjoy the rest of your Easter vacation. And remember to deactivate the deceleron once you enter Nina's house. Take the device and put it in the tree. I will have the scouts bring it back when they leave your things inside the trunk. Now hurry on home."

The girls approached the steps with their luminars. Piper turned for a brief moment and looked around.

"My stars, what a crazy adventure! What I have learned in one week!"

She wiped the moisture from her cheeks. Nina tugged on Piper's soiled shirt, and they both darted upward to another reality that would never be the same again.

Epilogue

Saturday, April 24 (morning)

Far below the tranquility of Holly Mills, two insidious figures stood. With boldness they entered the darkness of the Duruflàe Schism. Stopping at the midpoint, they faced each other's twisted hubris; the mighty trollian emperor broke the silence.

"It is to our advantage that it was left behind."

"Yes, the staff of power is safe and secure in Darkondusk," said the dark lord.

"Good. Very good."

"But the leader of all trolls must understand that the staff's power has been greatly diminished as it is far away from the gnomes' river. The closer it is to the Zander Zee, the more powerful it becomes."

"Nevertheless, it still possesses great power," insisted Shaptillicus.

"Which now, I might add, is at our disposal," offered Borok while wiping green slime from his repulsive mouth.

"Yes, great power! And at *our* disposal," said Shaptillicus who peered into the bloodshot orbs.

"So, I assume that the emperor has another diabolical plan to implement against these worthless gnomes?"

At first the troll refrained from any reply as he studied the features of his dubious ally from the south. Each distrusted the other, but each needed the other to achieve their desired ends. However, Shaptillicus had conceded to allow civility to restrain his deep disdain for the dark lord.

"What has occurred is only a setback, my dear Borok, only a minor setback," muttered the emperor as he leaned his bulky body against the sharp rocky wall.

"Ah, but of course. I must admit that it was rather clever of Tréfon to use the young uplanders in the rescue of his pathetic daughter," announced Borok. "But I wonder how the king knew to use humans?"

"Yes, humans." Shaptillicus leaned forward and breathed deeply. "And in time I will have my way with those two meddling females."

Borok rolled his repulsive head. His thick disgusting lips stretched to a mocking smile. "What now? What new scheme shall the great Shaptillicus use in order for us to establish an empire throughout *all* of Gilacia? I would assume that you have not capitulated to defeat."

The troll snorted, stiffened his mouth, and clenched his gray, callous fists. His pride prevented him from leaping forward and tearing his accomplice to shreds. "I do have connections in places other than this realm."

"Hmm! Am I to assume that you are involving the valley shadows from the west?"

"No! Not them or anyone of *this* world," groused the troll who ambled to the other side of the dark tunnel.

"Oh, then I presume you plan to enlist assistance from the Netranox? Or perhaps even the Jêhvaháer?" said Borok, who appeared more puzzled than curious.

"No."

"Well then, from where shall my opportunistic ally receive assistance?"

Pausing, the vengeful troll turned and faced the kandalarian. "Let us just say that I have a plan to overthrow the First Kingdom without much bloodshed."

"Without much bloodshed? How unlike you. But how is this even possible?" asked Borok.

The trollian leader drew an insidious smile, for in his mind he could hear distant throngs shouting aloud in unison, "All hail to Shaptillicus, ruler of the Gilatic Empire."

Shaptillicus grunted, turned and slowly walked back to the borders of his wicked empire. "Borok, you need to just, as they say, *reflect* on the matter for awhile. In any event, we shall have our revenge!"

Nina stared at the wall clock, wondering if she should make the telephone call to her best friend. Her main concern was secrecy: would any other family member accidentally pick up the receiver in the kitchen? She could not risk anyone other than Piper hearing the content of her conversation.

Her impulsiveness could not be contained by further logic. She shut her parents' bedroom door, lifted the handle, and dialed.

"Hello, Piper," she whispered into the mouthpiece. "Hey, can we get together soon? I really need to talk to you."

"Sure. My piano lesson's over at eleven o'clock, so let's meet up at Memorial Park at noon on our bikes."

Nina laughed. "Great! Say, let's make a picnic. Bring sandwiches, and I'll bring the drinks and snacks. I have so much to talk to you about."

"Me too. Hey, are your parents all right? I mean – you know," Piper said sheepishly.

"So far, so good; they don't suspect anything unusual. I just found it very hard to explain to them what I did while they were away from Holly Mills. Making up events for four days is not easy, right?"

"Tell me about it," said Piper. "I just about slipped a few times."

"Well, guess I'll see ya soon! Bye!"

Nina hung up the telephone and darted down the stairs. Her mother was making breakfast for the family, who slowly assembled around the kitchen table.

As the family partook of the eggs, bacon, and toast, Mr. and Mrs. Fithian exchanged comments about the Boston trip. Meanwhile, Nina's eyes glared across the table at Lance, who hummed the Davy Crockett theme while chewing with his mouth open. She turned her disapproving stare toward the kitchen window.

Like silica sand in gusty winds, Nina's mind whirled away with other, more meaningful thoughts. She imagined a safe and happy Princess Cirlaena walking about the splendid colonnades of the Royal Palace. She pictured Edip and Enver engaged in gnomen politics while strolling through the great halls of Spoleo. She envisioned herself onstage at Palmyra Pavilion, dazzling the audience with her ballet dancing. She could see it all so vividly.

But her heart ached and her countenance sank with interfering thoughts of a lost hero. What had become of the mysterious starling and his trusty cannoid?

So caught up in these speculations was she that her mother's calls went unheeded for several minutes. Only the confusing sounds of a new name haunted her mind like a menacing mantra with hidden admonition: "Rokáhn, Rokáhn, Rokáhn…"

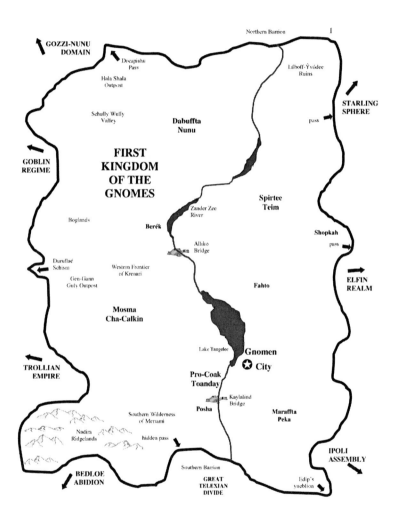

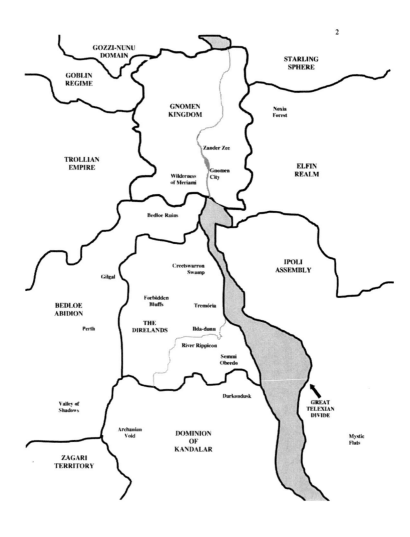

CPSIA information can be obtained
at www.ICGtesting.com
Printed in the USA
FSOW02n1458290916
25534FS

9 781613 791271